MW01174626

Collector's Edition

A collection of seven favorite
19th-century children's stories

Originally published in the 1800's
by the American Tract Society of New York

Grace & Truth Books
Sand Springs, Oklahoma

Collector's Edition

ISBN # 1-58339-124-x
Originally published in the 19th century
Current printing, Grace & Truth Books, 2005

Cover design by Ben Gundersen

Grace & Truth Books
3406 Summit Boulevard
Sand Springs, Oklahoma   74063
Phone: 918 245 1500

www.graceandtruthbooks.com

CONTENTS

PAGE

Farmer Goodwin's Rule   1

Ruth's Reward 21

Little Bill at the Pump 55

Who Is a Coward? 87

The Lost Lamb 109

The Good Shepherd 135

The Death of Emily 147

FARMER GOODWIN'S RULE

———————

"WELL, here you are, my boy, this fine May morning," said old Farmer Goodwin to Edward Finlay, as they met under the large oak that stands by the park fence; "—on your way to school as usual, I suppose, with your books in your hand, and all your lessons in your head; and I see you are in good time."

Edward and the old farmer had often met before, at the same hour and nearly at the same spot, so that they were becoming great friends. This morning Edward had some news to tell, of much importance to himself.

"Do you know, sir," said he, "I am going to a new school after the midsummer holidays? Father told me so last night. The school is a long way off, and I am to come home only twice a year. I shall have a great number of school-fellows; and there will be so many lessons to be learned, that I must not expect much time for play."

"That will be a change indeed!" said Farmer Goodwin, looking kindly at his young friend. "Such changes are pleasant at your age: and I have not forgotten how I felt when I was a boy like you. And yet I am pretty sure, Master Edward, that if you live to be a man, you will look back, with something like regret, to the days when you used to run across the fields to school.

"But in every state of life, and at every age," the old man went on to say, "we may find much to enjoy, and much to be thankful for—if, through grace, we are enabled rightly to receive every blessing and every trial, as it comes in love from our heavenly Father's hand. It is also true, that there is no state nor age which is free from temptation to sin; and the older you grow, my young friend, the more surely you will find this to be the case."

"I shall often think of you when I am away," said Edward; "and I hope I shall remember the good advice which you have given me at different times. I have not forgotten how you saved me from disgrace last year, by warning me against making Richard Ashton my friend. By this time I might have learned many of his bad ways; perhaps I should even have been turned out of the school the other day with him and Thomas Prescott, if you had not talked to me so about the danger of going with evil company."

"Glad and thankful should I be, my dear boy," said Farmer Goodwin, "if I could be of any use in helping you to keep the right road and the safe path. If my life is spared through the summer, I shall think of you many a time when I am taking my morning walk; and you may be sure I shall sometimes offer a prayer that God would bestow upon you the gift of His Holy Spirit, so that, amidst all your school-learning, you may not miss of learning the way to heaven. Mind your books,

Master Edward, and get as much knowledge as you can; for knowledge is a good thing indeed if it is used for the glory of God: but never forget that the salvation of your soul must be your chief concern: 'What shall it profit a man, if he shall gain the whole world, and lose his own soul? There is one good old rule which my father taught me when I was a lad; and if you take it with you to your new school, you may, with God's blessing, find it useful there. 'Never do any thing in the day which it will grieve you to think of at night.' Ponder this piece of advice; and whenever a sunshiny morning brings to your mind the days when you used to meet Farmer Goodwin, walking in the meadows, ask yourself whether you are trying to keep the old man's rule."

Edward thanked his kind friend: and then bade him good morning, and again set off to school. As he went along, he thought of the farmer's words: "Never do any thing in the day which it will grieve you to think of at night." "That is an easy rule, both to learn and to keep," said he to himself; "I should get on well at school, I am sure, if I were to meet with no harder task than this."

There wanted nearly three weeks to the holidays; yet it happened that, in all that time, Edward did not meet his friend again. There were some very rainy days, when the old man did not venture out; and then it was talked of in the village, that Farmer Goodwin was ill; and for many Sundays he was not seen in his place in the house of God. And so it was that the time came for Edward to go to his new school, without the two friends having seen each other since the bright May morning when they met under the old oak tree.

Edward was nearly twelve years old when he entered his new school. There were many boys of the same age with himself, and some who were much older. As he was cheerful and good-natured, had made pretty good progress in his learning, and could heartily join in a game at cricket, he soon gained the favour of both master and scholars, and had plenty of friends among the boys. Some of these friends were not likely to do him much good; but they were lively and fond of fun, and Edward did not wait, as he ought to have done, to see whether they were boys of good conduct in the school, before he joined their party. We should be kind to all, and willing to oblige; but it is only the good whom we should choose for our friends.

It was soon seen that Edward Finlay and Sydney Green were almost always together out of school-hours. If Farmer Goodwin could have overheard their talk on the play-ground one morning, when Edward had been at school about a month, he would have found that his warnings and advice were as needful as ever to his young friend.

"Why, Edward, my good fellow," said Sydney Green, "what was the matter with you last night? We had some fine fun at the other end of the school-room, and wanted you to join us; but there you sat with your book in your hand, never once coming near."

"You know it was Sunday evening," said Edward, in reply. At this, Sydney began to laugh. "Yes, I know it was Sunday," said he, "but I hope you are not like Harry Franklin and the other dull boys who do nothing but read the Bible and say their prayers. I hope you have too much spirit for that."

And here, reader, let me give you a word of caution. When you hear a boy talking in this way about "spirit," look upon it as a bad sign. Above all, if he speaks lightly of the Holy Scriptures and of prayer, be sure that such a boy is no fit companion for you.

"Come, tell me what you were reading last night?" asked Sydney, still laughing. "Was it the Bible, or a sermon-book that you brought from home?"

Edward blushed, and owned that it was the Bible. Why did he blush, as if he had been guilty of something wrong? It was because the wicked boy at his side had already taught him to feel ashamed of doing what was right. Observe the danger of a bad example. Edward had been brought up by pious parents, who had watched over him and prayed for him daily, and it was hoped that there was some love for the Saviour in his heart. Yet now, instead of lifting up his thoughts to God, who is ever near, and praying that he might be kept from evil, he listened to the sinful talk of Sydney Green, and soon began to join with him in laughing at those boys who were careful to keep holy the Sabbath day.

5

By-and-by Sydney began to speak about a plan which he had agreed upon with one of the day-scholars, of going early the next morning to gather nuts at some distance from the school. He asked Edward to go along with him, saying that it would be easy to get away without being seen, before the other boys were awake. "We shall be back by seven o'clock," said he, "with our pockets full of the finest nuts you ever saw. I went three or four times last autumn, and managed it so skillfully that I was never found out."

Now there was a very strict rule that the boys must not, on any account, go out of certain bounds without leave. Edward had been told this upon first coming to the school; and though he liked nuts, and liked still more the prospect of an early morning ramble, yet he was not willing to disobey. "I think it would be much better," said he, "if we were to ask leave to go to the woods next holiday afternoon. I don't want to get into disgrace."

"I tell you there is nothing to fear," said his bad adviser. "Besides, if we ask leave, of course all the other boys will expect to go, and then very few nuts will fall to our share. But I find I have been mistaken about you. I thought you were a boy of courage, till now; when I want you to join in a frolic, I find that you are as fearful as a mouse."

"Well, I will go this once," said Edward, "but you must never ask me again. I will go this once, just to show you that I am not afraid."

6

Poor Edward! he did not know that it would have been a far greater proof of true courage, if he had turned a deaf ear to the tempter, boldly choosing to do right. He had just given his assent, when Harry Franklin came up to them, with his hat in his hand, calling out in a loud and cheerful voice, "Who is ready for a game at cricket? There will be a good half-hour before the school-bell rings."

"Come here," said Sydney, "and I will tell you of some better fun than cricket. What do you say to going out nutting one of these fine mornings?"

"With all my heart," said Harry, looking very much pleased. "As you say, I should like it better than cricket. But when is it to be?"

"Whenever you please," was Sydney's reply, "for you need ask nobody's leave but your own."

"Then you know very well that I shall not go," said Harry, turning away quickly; and without seeming to heed the scornful laugh of his school-fellow, he was running on, when a sudden thought came into his mind which caused him to go up straight to Edward, who was trying to join in Sydney's laugh, though something told him that he was wrong. "Edward Finlay," said Harry, "do not let anyone persuade you to break the rules of the school. Sydney is older than you are, and ought to set you a good example, but I am afraid he will not do so; and some of us are very sorry that you have chosen him for your friend."

These words put Sydney into a great rage, so that he started forward to strike his school-fellow, but Harry stepped quietly aside. "I am not afraid of you, Sydney," said he; "though I don't want to quarrel with you, and you know I never fight; but Edward Finlay is a new boy, and therefore it is only right to put him on his guard. Come now, both of you to cricket; and if there has been any ill-will between us, let us forget it as soon as we can."

Edward was going to set off with Harry, but Sydney held him back. "You shall not belong to that set," said he, "or if you do, you must not expect to have me for a friend. And mind, after all that Harry Franklin has said, I shall insist that you keep your promise to-morrow morning."

"But will he not tell of us?" asked Edward. "You know it would be a bad thing for us if we should be found out."

"No fear of that," said Sydney, "unless you betray us by showing yourself a coward. He will think no more about it: besides, I did not tell him that we meant to go."

Edward said no more. He began to feel quite afraid of Sydney Green, and as soon as he could, he got away from him and went and sat down in the school-room by himself. He was very unhappy: he had never been so unhappy in his life, and yet he had not courage to do that which alone could bring peace to his mind. He had not courage to go to Sydney Green, and tell him that he would not be a partaker in his sin.

Some children may think this strange; but others know very well what it is to let a fellow-creature have such power over them, that they fear his displeasure more than they fear to break the commands of God. Yet a little thought might show them how foolish and sinful is this fear: for what is the anger of a fellow-creature when compared with the wrath of Him who is able to destroy both soul and body in hell? If Edward had gone boldly up to Sydney to tell him that he repented of his promise, the utmost that this bad boy could have done would have been to sneer at him and call him a few hard names: how much better to bear these than the Divine displeasure, and the reproaches of conscience! Whoever may be against us, we should never be afraid of doing our duty; we should never be ashamed to show that it is our desire to obey our Saviour and keep His commandments. We must be bold and fearless in doing right, however others may try to oppose and prevent us. This is called moral courage; and it is courage of the highest and noblest kind.

But you will say that it is not easy to act in this way. Perhaps you may tell me that you have tried do so in vain. I am ready to agree with you that it is not an easy thing. But what makes it so difficult? It is the wickedness of our hearts, which leads us to think lightly of sin, and to desire the praise of men rather than the honour which cometh from God only. We should pray that God would help us by His Holy Spirit to resist all temptation to sin, and to resolve that, whatever others may do, we will be the servants of the Lord.

During all that day, though Edward tried to seem the same as on other days, there was a secret burden on his mind which he could not get rid of, either in lessons or play. When night came, just as they were leaving the school-room after prayers, Sydney Green stepped up to him, and whispered, "I shall call for you to-morrow morning in good time."

Edward made no reply; but went up-stairs with a heavy heart, feeling that he was about to do wrong, and wishing to draw back, but still not daring to do so, from his foolish dread of what Sydney Green might say. When he lay down in bed, the thought of home came into his mind, with the advice which his parents had given to him before they parted. And then, too, for the first time since that bright May morning, he remembered the good old rule of Farmer Goodwin, "Never do any thing in the day which it will grieve you to think of at night." He thought of it for the first time. Ah! if he had kept it in mind from day to day, and that without trusting in his own strength, but seeking for the grace of Christ, he would not have been so easily persuaded to join in another's sin.

After passing some restless hours upon his pillow, Edward at last made the resolve which he ought to have made at first, that, let Sydney say what he might, when he came to his bed-side in the morning, he would tell him how unhappy he had been on account of his sinful promise, and firmly refuse to go. Having made up his mind to this, his trouble seemed to leave him, and he soon fell fast asleep.

The sun had scarcely risen when the door of Edward's chamber was softly opened, and Sydney stole into the room. Edward started up the moment that he felt a hand upon his shoulder; and Sydney bade him be quick, but said that he must be quiet also, lest the other boys should awake.

"I do not intend to go with you, Sydney," said Edward. "I have been very unhappy ever since I gave my consent to your plan, and I should be still more unhappy if I were to go."

"No matter for that," replied Sydney; "you have given me your word, and you must keep it, if you wish to be thought a boy of honour."

"No," said Edward, firmly, "it was wrong, I know, to make such a promise, but it would be worse to keep it. Indeed, I cannot go."

"Well," said Sydney, "I did not expect that this would be the end of all your friendship. And when we might go so easily too, and nobody be at all the wiser! It is as pleasant a morning as you ever saw; and I'll be bound that Fred Parkyns, with his nut-hook, is already looking out for us at the grove. Come, Edward, act like a man. What harm can there be in slipping out for an hour or two, just to gather a few nuts?"

"Are you sure that we can get away without being seen?" asked Edward, his firmness giving way as he saw the early sunshine, and thought of the brown clusters hanging on the hazel-boughs.

"Oh yes! we can let ourselves out at my window, for it is not very far from the ground, and no one else sleeps in that room, you know. When we come back again some of the doors will be open, as the servants will be about; and we can run quietly up-stairs. The rest will be easy enough, for the boys will think we have been up early at our books. So make haste—there is no time to lose, and besides, I long to be off."

Did old Farmer Goodwin's rule again come into Edward's mind? However this might be, the temptation was too strong for him, and he trusted in his own heart: he rose and dressed himself quickly, then crept softly out of the room; and, as Sydney had truly said, his window was not far from the ground, so that in a few minutes the two boys were standing safe on the green turf below. It was easy to climb over the garden wall; and they were soon on their way to the woods, talking merrily as they went along, so that Edward forgot all concern about doing wrong, and thought of nothing but the amusement of the present hour.

A nutting party in the early autumn is a very pleasant thing, as everybody knows; but then, to be fully enjoyed, the heart and the conscience should both be free from care. When this is not the case, we may sometimes forget our trouble for a short time, but the thought of it soon returns. When sin is allowed to enter into our pleasures, "even in laughter the heart is sorrowful, and the end of that mirth is heaviness." Edward began to feel it so before he had been long in the woods; but his two companions were more hardened in disobedience, and he tried to talk as loudly and to seem as happy as they.

The time flew fast; and though the ripe brown nuts hung thick on many a bough, they had not gathered all they wished for, before it was needful to set off on their return. The sun, rising higher and higher, should have warned them to hasten on; but they loitered still in the woods, tempted first by one rich cluster and then by another, so that when they reached the high road, and were really setting off in good earnest, it was much nearer seven o'clock than they supposed. They both began to feel alarmed; and Sydney, hurrying on, called out sharply to Edward to make haste saying that he alone would be to blame if they should be found out. Poor Edward thought this rather unjust; but he said nothing, only doing his best to keep up with Sydney, who was allowed to be one of the fastest runners in the school.

But now came trouble upon trouble. Edward's foot struck violently against a stone, and down he fell; Sydney still running on, never stopping to inquire if he were hurt or to give him help. He tried to pick himself up again, caring nothing for the bruises on his hands; but, to his dismay, he found that one ankle gave him such pain that he could scarcely put his foot to the ground. He felt sure that he could not walk to the school without some assistance and support: yet Sydney never once looked back, and though Edward called to him, he did not seem to hear. At this moment the village clock struck seven.

Sydney heard the sound, and suddenly stopped, for he knew that their misconduct would now certainly be found out. Edward again called to him for help; and this time he went back, but grumbling all the way, and showing no signs of pity for his school-fellow, who was now suffering much pain and distress both of body and mind. It is not those who have tempted us to evil that are most ready to feel for us and to show us kindness when trouble comes; for sin hardens the heart and makes it selfish, and those who delight in it care little for others, being only "lovers of their own selves."

And now it is time to speak of what was passing in the school. It was usual for the boys to meet in the school-room, on the ringing of a bell, at seven o'clock, when a chapter was read, and a prayer offered for the Divine blessing through the day. After this, they had breakfast, and then, in fine weather, went into the play-ground, where they remained until the bell again rang at nine, and the business of school began.

When Sydney and Edward were missed from their proper places there was a close inquiry made, and the other boys were desired to say if they knew any thing about them. Harry Franklin was one of the last who would choose to become a tell-tale; but after waiting a little while to hear if anyone else could speak upon the matter, he thought it was his duty in this case to repeat what Sydney had said to him the morning before. The good master looked grave and sad when he heard this news, and said there could be no doubt that the two boys were gone to the woods. He made a few remarks on the sin of disobedience and the evils to which it led; and, as they were kneeling down to pray, he expressed his hope that the boys would all join him, with their hearts, in asking that the Holy Spirit would take away all wickedness from among them, for the sake of Jesus Christ, who died upon the cross, that we might be cleansed from every sin.

It was nearly eight o'clock when Sydney and Edward made their appearance at one end of the play-ground, where they stood for a minute or two, looking foolish and ashamed, as well they might. Edward could not support himself, but was leaning upon Sydney's shoulder; and the long walk had given him such great pain, that he could now think of nothing else.

There they stood, at one end of the play-ground, with the eyes of all their school-fellows turned upon them, and seeing their disgrace. Harry Franklin was the first to come forward with a kind word. "Tell the truth, Edward," said he, "and do not try to hide any thing from our master. He will forgive you, if you are really sorry for having done wrong."

15

"Oh! I am sorry, indeed I am sorry!" cried Edward, bursting into tears. He could not say any more, because the pain of his foot was so great; but he did not complain, for he knew that he had deserved it all.

And now you may guess what followed when the master was told that the truants had returned. Edward's sufferings were already so severe that no other punishment was needed: he was therefore taken to bed, and the doctor was sent for without delay. Poor Edward! He had to remain in bed more than a week; and it was a long, long time before he could play at leap-frog or foot-ball, or join in another game at cricket.

While Edward lay on his bed of pain, he had many sad hours alone, during which he thought over his bad conduct, and grieved for it, (it was hoped,) with an humble and penitent heart. He felt that he was a very sinful child; and as he had been so soon led astray, he was afraid to make any promises of amendment, because he knew that a heart so weak and wicked as his was not to be trusted any more. He prayed to Jesus for pardon, but he had many fears that He would not hear him on account of his sins. Edward's kind master, who came to see him every day, talked to him about the evil of sin and the grace of Christ to repenting sinners, and told him where to look for many sweet promises of forgiveness in the word of God. Edward learned a number of such texts as these: "This is a faithful saying, that Christ Jesus came into the world to save sinners."* "The blood of Jesus Christ His Son cleanseth us from all sin."† "Him that cometh to Me I will in no wise cast out."‡

By degrees he began to feel some hope that his prayers would be heard, since the Bible so plainly says, that Christ died for sinners, and will have mercy upon all who believe in Him. He also earnestly asked that a new heart might be given to him, and a new spirit be put within him, for the sake of Christ his Saviour; that so he might love the way of holiness and hate the paths of sin. Reader, whatever may be your age, you are by nature a sinner, and have need to seek for pardon and a change of heart. Remember that the time is short. Life is uncertain, and death may be nearer than you think. Oh! ask yourself, are you prepared to live in the service of Christ, or to die in His favour?

The violation of this rule of the school, in this single instance, might seem a very small matter to make such much ado about, but we must remember that the state of a child's heart and his readiness to yield to temptation, are as clearly seen in a single act of disobedience to the command of a parent or teacher, as in many and bold transgressions. It was this that gave so much importance to Edward's fault and required such serious notice.

Harry Franklin spent many hours by Edward's bedside, and to him the unhappy boy

---

* I Tim. i. 15.
† I John i. 7.
‡ John vi. 37.

17

could tell all his troubles and freely open his heart. From this time they became great friends; and theirs was true friendship, for they wished to help each other to do right, and were both afraid of sin. As for Sydney Green, his disobedience was severely punished by their master, nor did Fred Parkyns, (the day-scholar,) escape; but as no great improvement was seen in their conduct while they remained at school, you will be glad to learn that Edward did not become intimate with them again.

At the Christmas holidays, Farmer Goodwin kindly asked his young friend to pay him a visit one day, when it came out that Edward had not always kept the farmer's good old rule. Farmer Goodwin heard his story with much patience.

"Well, my boy," said he, at last, "a good rule is not to be despised, any more than a good resolve; yet we shall find that neither are worth much if we try to keep them in our own strength. We must put our trust in God, and pray to him for grace. Then what is hard will become easy; for His grace is sufficient for us; and though we can do nothing of ourselves, yet we may do all things through Christ, Who gives us strength."

HYMN

Among the deepest shades of night,
Can there be one who sees my way?
Yes; God is like a shining light,
That turns the darkness into day.

When every eye around me sleeps,
May I not sin without control?
No; for a constant watch He keeps
On every thought of every soul.

If I could find some cave unknown,
Where human feet had never trod,
Yet there I could not be alone,
On every side there would be God.

He smiles in heaven, He frowns in hell.
He fills the earth, the air, the sea;
I must within His Presence dwell,
I cannot from His anger flee.

Yet I may flee; He shows me where;
To Jesus Christ He bids me fly;
And while I seek for pardon there,
There's only mercy in His eye.

THE END

RUTH'S REWARD

CHAPTER I

THE OLD FARM-HOUSE

"O Lord, how manifold are Thy works!
in wisdom hast Thou made them all: the
earth is full of Thy riches." - Psalm civ. 24.

ONCE upon a time, in an old-fashioned farmhouse, lived a little girl whom we will call Ruth. Very likely many of you who are reading this have been in the summer time to a farm-house; and perhaps you have played round its old-fashioned doors and windows, or looked into its many out-buildings and barns, to say nothing of the pleasures of seeing the young life about the farm in the form of chickens, ducks, pigs, lambs, calves, and kittens. You have, too, enjoyed the lovely farm-house butter and fresh eggs for breakfast and tea; and have thought how very nice it must be to live at a farm-house, or, at any rate, in the country. Well, it is very nice to be in God's open country, and see the wonderful handiwork of God around us, not only in the trees and fields, but also in the marvellous instinct He has given to all His creatures, and one is ready to exclaim:

"His glories blaze all nature round,
And strike the gazing sight;
Thro' skies and seas, and solid ground,
With pleasure and delight.

Infinite strength and equal skill
Shine through the worlds abroad;
Our souls with vast amazement fill,
And speak the builder—God!"

The house where our young friend was born
was surrounded with tall trees and it was situated in
a very pretty part of the county of Sussex. It was a
real old-fashioned place, with ever so many doors
and little windows; and in the living room there was
a wonderful fire-place, not at all like our fire-places
which have grates to place the fire in, but what was
called a "down" fire; that means, the fire was all on
the hearth; and if, when there was no fire, you had
looked up the large chimney, you would have seen
the sky. You could put huge logs of wood on the
fire at one time; and on either side of the fire-place
there were cosy little places, called "chimney
corners." Ruth used to love to sit in these chimney
corners, with her own cat, named Joe, in her arms,
and think and imagine all sorts of things in her
active little brain, as she watched the flames and
sparks go up the chimney. She was particularly fond
of the old cat, and I believe that when it died it was
properly buried, and all the children of the family

followed it to its grave. At other times she would sit on her father's knee, and learn her letters out of the big old Bible.

At the time our story opens she was about twelve years old, and though living in such a beautiful part of God's earth, she was not without the trial and troubles which, more or less, all boys and girls are born unto. About nine years before this time she could just remember seeing her own dear mother lie dead.

Of course, she was too young to understand very much. She knew her mother had gone to heaven, and she would sometimes watch the clouds to see if she could see her once more. Like other children, she was very pleased with her new clothes when her mother died; but her good old grandmother put her hand on her little head, and said, "Ah, my dear, you little know what it is to be left without a mother's care."

Ruth had a kind father, but some time after her mother's death he married again, and I am sorry to say this stepmother was not always very kind to her. By this time she had several other brothers and sisters younger than herself, of whom she was very fond, and loved to play with them in the orchard and garden.

There is also one other sad thing I must tell you about Ruth. She was born with crippled feet! In addition to this, she often suffered much during the winter from broken chilblains, which, not being properly attended to, made her poor feet worse; so that, as she grew older, she was less able to run or walk about than other children. Oh, dear young friends, how much we have to thank God for, if we have health and strength, and can see and speak and hear; and yet how little we think of these mercies. There is so much sadness in the world, and wherever we go we may see it; and I am sure you have heard many times the account of the Fall of man, after God had made Adam and Eve, and had placed them in a beautiful garden, where there was no sorrow or suffering because there was no sin. God told them that they might freely eat of all the trees of the garden, except of one tree. We cannot imagine how great was the happiness of Adam and Eve, with everything around them to add to their comfort. All the animals were under their control, and the earth brought forth food for them to eat. There was no anger, or lying, or any other sin there to cause pain or sorrow; and to crown, as it were, their happiness, God walked and talked with them in the garden.

Then the Bible tells us how Satan, in the form of a serpent, tempted Eve, and she took of the forbidden fruit, and ate of it, and gave some to Adam, and he did eat. After this, the sad account goes on to tell how they were ashamed, and hid themselves amongst the trees of the garden; but neither they nor we can hide from God, Who searches the heart, and even knows every thought as well as every action. He condemned the guilty pair, and they had to leave the beautiful garden, and were never allowed to enter it again. God, however, in His mercy, promised, even in that garden, that He would send them and their children a Saviour, even the Lord Jesus Christ.

Perhaps some of you may have thought that you would not have acted just like Adam and Eve; but if any of my readers think this, let him or her remember the many times they have done that which was wrong; and then they will not be able to say that they are better than Adam. How much, dear boys and girls, we need each and all to seek for pardon through the Lord Jesus Christ, Who alone can cleanse and keep us from sin.

CHAPTER II

SHOVERS GREEN CHAPEL

"Lord, I have loved the habitation of
Thy house, and the place where Thine
honour dwelleth." - Psalm xxvi. 1.

"RUTH, you shall not go to Chapel to-day!"
said a harsh-speaking woman.

"But, Mother, I do so want to go," said Ruth,
in quiet tones.

"You little hypocrite! going to chapel,
making out you are so good!" replied Mrs. Ellis.

"Well, Mother, I really have done all I can,
and I am going to take Mary and Bill along with me,
so they will be out of your way; and the baby is
asleep."

"It is all very well for you to talk! I have had
enough of this canting; it is only to make people
think you are so good!" and with that Mrs. E.
slammed the door in a terrible passion.

Poor little Ruth, what should she do? She had
tried that morning to do everything she possibly
could, that she might be able to go to chapel, though
it was so much trouble for her to walk about; and
now there was all this upset and passion. You must
not think Ruth was different from other boys and
girls. Oh, no! She felt very angry and hurt at her
step-mother's unjust remarks, and as she hobbled
along the road to the Chapel, a great battle raged

within her heart. The Chapel was only about a quarter-of-a-mile from her home, so she could manage to get there. Some years before this time— she was now about twelve years old—there had been placed in Ruth's heart by the Holy Spirit, a desire after God and the people of God. She could not understand the strange feelings herself, but she knew that deep down in her heart there was a desire to go to Chapel and to know about God. When quite young, these lines of a hymn seemed spoken to her heart:

> "Oft as the bell, with solemn toll,
> Speaks the departure of a soul;
> Let each one ask himself, 'Am I
> Prepar'd, should I be call'd to die?'"

And from that time there was in her young heart a longing to be prepared for death. Sometimes she had been afraid of going to bed, in case she never woke up again. At another time when she was in school, and the class were having a Scripture lesson on the 25th chapter of Matthew, it affected her very much. You have heard read that wonderful Parable of the Sheep and the Goats, when the Lord Jesus will come in all His glory, and divide the "sheep"— those who have been made to feel their need of Jesus to save them and wash them from their sins in His blood—from the "goats"—those who have not prayed for their sins to be forgiven. We read that Jesus will set the "sheep" on His right hand and the "goats" on His left hand. As the teacher was telling them of these solemn things, poor Ruth was afraid she would be one of the "goats," and that she would hear those awful words, "Depart from Me, ye cursed, into everlasting fire, prepared for the devil and his angels," and she fainted right away.

Also, when some little playmates died from diphtheria, she was very troubled. She knew there was a place called heaven, where good people went when they died; and she knew there was a dreadful place, called hell, and she had been told sometimes, when she was naughty, that she would go there. In the field there were some sand-pits, and she used to wonder if deep down there was the place. She was very nervous in thunderstorms, and would run and hide in some dark corner. Once there was a terrible storm, and two horses were killed, and she feared that the end of the world had come.

Ruth, on the other hand, was sometimes helped and felt encouraged by having answers to her prayers. Once she prayed to God that it might not rain when she was going to some special treat, and it was wonderful how the weather cleared, and she was able to go.

One day she asked her father if she could be baptized and confirmed at the Church, as she thought she would then be more ready for heaven; but he very kindly said to her, "That would not do you any good, my maid. God must change the heart." How Ruth tried to be a good girl! but, alas! she had to learn that she was a sinner, and needed nothing less than the precious blood of Christ to wash her from her sin, and make her "whiter than snow." What a great blessing it is, dear readers, to be taught to pray from our hearts:

"Prepare me, gracious God
To stand before Thy face;
Thy Spirit must the work perform,
For it is all of grace."

CHAPTER III

A SPECIAL SUNDAY

"For the needy shall not alway be forgotten;
the expectation of the poor shall not perish for ever."
Psalm ix. 18.

AND now we must return to where we left Ruth at the beginning of the previous chapter. As she slowly made her way along the road on that beautiful summer morning—you must remember she was only a young girl—she came to the conclusion that, after all, it would be better for her not to go to Chapel any more against her mother's wishes, and that she would stay at home. So she decided that, from this day forth, it was best she cease from being present at the services, and asked God to forgive her if she did not go again. This was a great grief to her, for she looked forward so much to Sunday, and often on that morning she would wake up early, and sing the little hymn:

"This is the day when Christ arose
So early from the dead;
Why should I keep my eyelids closed
And waste my hours in bed?"

There was a dear old lady at the Chapel who always would make room in her seat for Ruth and the children. How well it is when those who are

31

older speak kindly to the young, and pray for them that they may, if God's will, be raised up as "a seed to serve Him" in the days to come!

Ruth had not much time to read her Bible, which she loved so much; and even that week her mother had said that she would burn it. I do not want my little readers to think that it is right for them to disobey their parents. The Bible plainly says, "Children *obey* your parents in the Lord: for this is right;" but when it comes to a matter of serving God, we must remember also the words of Jesus, "Whosoever loveth father and mother more than Me, is not worthy of Me."

Well, Ruth got to the little country Chapel that morning just as they were singing the first hymn. The minister then read and prayed as usual, and gave out his text, which was, "Fear not, for I am with thee." In the course of his sermon Mr. Jones, for that was the minister's name, was led to speak of some of the hardships he had passed through in his young days. He had been a poor workhouse boy, and was afterwards placed with a farmer who feared not God. At that time Mr. Jones loved his Bible, and tried to read it when he could find an opportunity; but he was very much afraid of his master, so he used to hide it under the straw by the horses' feet in the stable, or in the manger.

You can imagine poor Ruth's feeling and her surprise as she heard this, for that very week, she had been so troubled to know where to hide her Bible and hymnbook, as her mother had told the other children to tell her if they saw Ruth reading them, and she would have the books destroyed. Ruth had wrapped them up very carefully, and hidden them up in the chimney in one of the bedrooms, where they did not have a fire. It seemed so wonderful to her that the minister should speak as he did that Sunday morning. Of course, he knew nothing about her trial or her temptation. She felt from that time that she *must* go to Chapel, whatever might happen; and she returned home that morning with a stronger desire than ever to be found in the House of God whenever she could.

Perhaps some of you may think the services at Chapel are rather long and dull, and that there is not much said by the minister that you can understand; but you must remember that God sees children when they are in His house, and sometimes He speaks to them by His ministers. When any seek Him, and desire to hear His voice, it is because He will be to them the Good Shepherd, Who loves the lambs as well as the sheep.

The writer well remembers two children who once were quarrelling, and, what made it more sad, it was on a Sunday morning. The little girl was very aggravating, and the little boy said in a passion, "I hate you!" The girl at once replied, "It says in the Bible, 'Whosoever hateth his brother is a murderer.'" The boy argued that those words were not in the Bible, but the girl still said that they were. However, when they got to Chapel that morning, the old minister read from the First Epistle of John, chapter 3, in which is the verse: "Whosoever hateth his brother is a murderer," and made some remarks upon it. The boy and girl never forgot the incident, and God seemed very near to them that Sunday. Children, do not forget that God's eye is ever on you, and that He sees all your thoughts and actions. How very different our lives would be if we could remember more often that wonderful text, "Thou God seest me"!

CHAPTER IV

THE GOOD SHEPHERD'S CARE

"For thus saith the LORD GOD; Behold, I
even I, will both search My sheep, and seek them out"
Ezekiel xxxiv. 11.

"**I** HAVE some news for you, Ruth," said her father one day.

"Oh, what is it, father?" Ruth enquired. "Is it good news?"

"Well, my little maid, how would you like to go and live with your Aunt Maria? She wants someone to help her with the children, and I wondered if you would like to go?"

"Oh, yes, father, I would!"

"Well, you shall go. Uncle Samuel will be here in about two weeks with a horse and cart, and will take you over, if you are sure you would like to go. We shall have to get you a few things together, and try and have a pair of shoes made for you." This last item was very difficult, as poor Ruth's feet did not get any better, but rather worse. However, Ruth was very *pleased* at the prospect, for she knew one thing about her aunt which made her feel glad, and that was, she attended the Chapel at Heathfield. Now she felt there would be no difficulty in getting to Chapel; for she knew, too, that her uncle had a horse and buggy, which were used chiefly on Sundays to take them to Chapel. How much Ruth thought of, and longed for, the time to come when she should go to her aunt's! Things had not been much better at home lately, and like us all, when things are not comfortable, she thought how nice it would be to get away. I should tell you, that though she was so crippled, she was not a lazy girl. No, she loved work; but her greatest difficulty was to get to the House of God. Sometimes she would slip into the prayer-meeting at the Chapel, when she was out shopping, and would sit on the gallery stairs. Being still so young, she could not understand some of the things that were said; but the Good Shepherd did not forget His little lamb, and there were many times when Ruth had a blessing, which made her long still more to be able to get to the House of God. In fact, sometimes that seemed to be the great object of her life. She could truthfully say with the Psalmist, "How amiable are Thy tabernacles, O Lord of hosts!" and again, "I had rather be a doorkeeper in the house of my God, than to dwell in the tents of wickedness" (Psalm lxxxiv. 1,10).

At another time, when out in the field with some of the children, as they were playing together, and Ruth was sitting watching, a sweet feeling came over her, and she believed that the Lord would fulfil her desire, and that she would know more of those blessed realities she so desired to possess. Truly the word of old was verified in her case, "Then shall we know, if we follow on to know the Lord." She was often ridiculed and told not to pull a long face or look so miserable, but she did not mind that.

Sometimes there was a verse of a hymn that just seemed to suit her case. One day she came across the hymn which begins:

> "O Lord, I would delight in Thee,
> And on Thy care depend;
> To Thee in every trouble flee,
> My best, my only Friend!"

and she was so anxious not to forget this, that she wrote the number of it (247, Gadsby's) on the wall of her room. What an unspeakable mercy it is to have Jesus for our Friend! He has a sweet name in the Bible, though it was given to Him by His enemies: "The Friend of sinners." He came down from heaven to die for poor sinners, as the little hymn says:

> "Jesus, Who lived above the sky,
> Came down to be a man and die;
> And in the Bible we may see
> How very good He used to be."

He is a "Friend that loveth at all times." Our earthly friends may die, or fail us when we most need them. Do you feel that you need Jesus to be your Friend?

"How happy is the child who hears
Instruction's warning voice,
And who celestial wisdom makes
His early, only choice!"

CHAPTER V

LIFE IN A NEW HOME

"And Ruth said, Intreat me not to leave
thee ... thy people shall be my people,
and thy God my God."—Ruth i. 16.

WELL, the two weeks came to an end at last, and Ruth's uncle arrived; the little box was packed up, and Ruth left her home to live with her uncle. She was sorry to leave her dear father and her little brothers and sisters, but the thought of going to her aunt who went to Chapel, soon comforted her; and, like it would be to all other children, the fact of going somewhere fresh was pleasing to her. It was a long ride to her uncle's home, but the good horse soon brought them along; and when Ruth went to her little bed that night, she thanked God for making a way for her out of her difficulties, and for bringing her to her uncle's home. How little she knew what the future would be, and it was her mercy, as well as ours, that "God holds the key of all unknown." She was told she must not write home too often, or expect letters from home, as there was two pence to pay for every letter carried to the farm.

Our little friend was now about thirteen years of age. She was not very big for her years, and looked so delicate, that she seemed quite unsuited for the hard work of a farmhouse, with its many duties and busy life. Ruth's aunt had several little children, and there was plenty to do with butter-churning, and baking bread and other things in the great oven. Then there was the milk to set for cream, and to sell. But, as I have said before, she was very industrious, and fond of children, and the busy days passed quickly. Then there was always Sunday to look forward to; and at that time the beloved Mr. George Mockford was the Pastor of Heathfield Chapel. Many times Ruth was helped by his encouraging remarks to young seekers, and she found the gospel to be a precious balm to her wounded spirit. She felt that she was a sinner in God's sight and needed a Saviour, and as the minister exalted a precious Christ, it was food to her soul.

This knowledge that she was a sinner was not only when she was in the house of God, but she felt it also when unable to get there, it being three miles from the farmhouse, and somebody had always to stay at home with the little babies. When this was the case, our young friend would try and get away somewhere quiet and pray to God.

One Sunday, when in great distress, and longing to know that her sins were forgiven and all her faults pardoned, she went away at this particular time to a secret place for prayer, and there the Lord spoke to her. I do not mean in a voice that could be heard by others, but by His Holy Spirit He spoke to her heart; and the sweet words of the poet were brought to her mind:

"Payment God cannot twice demand,
First at my bleeding Surety's hand,
And then again at mine."

Oh, the beauty she saw in those lines, as she thought of the Lord Jesus taking the place of poor sinners, and suffering on the cross instead of them! and she ventured to hope that "her guilt was there," and that the Lord Jesus suffered to put away her sins. Oh, how she felt to love Him! and the time passed so quickly, that she was afraid something might have happened to the children she was left to mind. She hurried back to them, and was glad to find they were safe. After a time, Mr. Mockford, hearing about her from the friends, would sometimes write to her, and send it by an old friend; and this is how it was addressed to her: "Ruth, travelling in the path between hope and fear."

You must not forget that our little friend was still very crippled. I expect some of you would have grumbled very much if you had half as much to do as she had in her aunt's house, and you probably have the full use of your limbs; but Ruth was very persevering, and it is often astonishing what can be done if one tries; but for all this she often had great difficulty in getting about, and would go up and down stairs on her knees, and would kneel to wash the dishes or the clothes. It was difficult to get boots made to fit her, and though this happened not so very long ago, there were not the conveniences and helps for poor cripples then as there are now.

But Ruth soon found to her astonishment and sorrow that she had more trouble before her. Her aunt, strange to say, no sooner found that Ruth wanted to go to Chapel, than she opposed it, and would often put obstacles in the way of her going; and, as I have said, there were several young children to mind. Well, at this particular time about which I am writing, it had been that week after week Ruth had looked forward to going to Chapel, and had been disappointed. It was now six Sundays, and she felt very, very sad about it. You all know what it is to expect to go somewhere very nice, and then not to be able to go, so you can understand something of what Ruth felt. However, her uncle, seeing her sad face, as he drove off to Chapel on the sixth Sunday, said, "Never mind, Ruth, you shall go next Sunday. I will see to that." This pleased her very much, for she knew her uncle would keep his word; and she did what I expect you have all done sometimes, when you have wanted a special time to come ever so much—she began to count the days, and I am sure Ruth longed for Sunday to come, but she was to have another time of trial to pass through.

Saturday morning came, and she thought, "Only one more day, and I shall go to Chapel!" but when her uncle came in as usual to have his lunch that morning, he looked across at her as she was washing up the milk pails, and said, "Well, my girl, I am afraid you will not be able to go to Chapel after all, to-morrow, for Darling has got the influenza!" Darling was the name of the horse he drove in the little buggy that took them to Chapel. Ruth nearly dropped the pail she was wiping, and all the colour went from her face. "Oh, uncle," she said, "I am sorry!" He went into the kitchen to have his lunch, and really felt very sorry for his little niece, for he knew that she worked very hard and had little change or pleasure.

Soon he thought of a bright idea, and, calling her, said, "Ruth, I have been thinking of the old pony out in the field. She is right away from all the other horses, and is quite well. We could have her to-morrow, if you would like to clean the harness."

"Oh, yes, I will clean the harness!" said Ruth eagerly. "I don't mind doing that, if you will bring it in."

"All right, my little maid," replied her uncle, "you shall have it."

Now if we could have seen Ruth's face, what a change would have been noticed! It was now bright and cheerful, and like sunshine after rain. That Saturday was a busy day—baking in the big brick oven, and many other things, so that the hours went by quickly, and it had struck ten by the old grandfather clock before Ruth could touch the harness. The family had all gone to bed, leaving Ruth in the big old wash-house to get on with her task; she did not mind this, although she could hear the rats running about and trying to get into the corn tubs at the end of the wash-house. She worked away with a good will, until every buckle and button of that old pony's harness shone like gold, and every leather strap was blacked and polished like a boot. She hung it up in the usual place to dry, and just as the clock struck the hour of midnight, crept upstairs to bed.

She was very tired, but happy at the prospect of going to the House of God the next day, and soon fell asleep.

CHAPTER VI

A GREAT DISAPPOINTMENT

"God moves in a mysterious way
His wonders to perform."

SUNDAY morning dawned bright and fair, and our little friend was up in time, dressing the children and eagerly looking forward to going to Chapel! But listen! she hears her uncle calling to her from below. She hurries to the top of the stairs, and calls out, "What is the matter?"

He hesitates for a time, and then calls out, "It is a mercy we were not all burnt to death!"

"Oh, dear! whatever can have happened?"

"Well, that harness you cleaned last night is so burnt that we cannot possibly use it! I have been looking at it, to see if I could possibly tie it together somehow, so that we could use it, but it is impossible."

When Ruth had finished cleaning the harness she hung it up over the wood which was put by for the next day's fire, and by some means the hot embers from the brick oven fell on the wood and set it afire, and so burnt the harness; but the strange thing was that nothing else was destroyed. This was a terrible blow to her, and she felt as if she must sink through the floor. It was all over now, and all her prayers, and longings, and desires to go to Chapel were all in vain. How she finished dressing

45

the children, or how she got the breakfast ready, she did not know—her heart seemed as if it would break. Perhaps some of you may think that Ruth made a great fuss about going to Chapel on that particular Sunday, but I believe God Himself put that strong desire in her heart to go to His house, that He might display His wonderful power in her. We see instances of this in the Word of God, though in a far greater way. God puts the desire and prayer in the heart, and then works out His own purposes contrary to human plans or expectations. And so Ruth found it, as we shall see in the next chapter.

I might also mention the case of Mary Jones, the Welsh girl, who many years ago had such a desire to possess a Bible of her own, that she saved up all the money she had for a long time, and then walked more than twenty miles with bare feet to where she thought she would be able to buy one. Her disappointment was great when she was told that there was not a Bible left, for they were scarce in those days. This led the good minister, Mr. Charles, of Bala, to give her his Bible; and soon after, when Mary's love to the Word of God became known, a Society was formed, and money given, so that Bibles might be printed in the Welsh language, and then poor people could obtain them much more easily and cheaply than before. Thus God honoured and blessed the love that Mary Jones had to His Word.

CHAPTER VII

A WONDERFUL JOURNEY

"Then shall the lame man leap as an hart,
and the tongue of the dumb sing."
Isaiah xxxv. 6.

To return to our story. We left our friend
Ruth in great distress, owing to the harness having
been burnt, and that therefore she would be unable
to go to Chapel that day; but after the breakfast was
over, and her aunt was preparing to go, Ruth said:

"Aunt, I feel as if I *must* go to Chapel. You
will have to lock me in the house if you want me to
stay at home to-day."

"What is the use of talking like that? You
know you cannot get there," replied her aunt.

"Well, aunt, I feel I will try and walk there."

"You know you cannot walk; it is three
miles."

"I don't know, aunt, but I feel that I shall not
have to sit down on the road," replied Ruth.

"Well, I think you are nothing less than a
hypocrite. You make enough fuss over getting about
the house, and then to think of walking to Chapel! It
is ridiculous; I have no patience with you!" and her
aunt rushed out of the room very angry.

Poor Ruth! it did *seem* a foolish thing for her
to think of doing, and she felt that her aunt was
quite justified in what she said; but somehow or
other she felt she *must* try, and strange to say, her

aunt consented to stay with the children. She went upstairs to get ready in great fear and trembling; and as she entered her bedroom it was suggested to her—I believe by God: "Get some wadding, and pad your shoes!" which was a thing she had not done before. So she got her shoes out to put them on, and chose two odd ones, as one foot was easier in a shoe of one pair, and the other foot in a shoe of the other pair. She took some wadding, and padded her shoes, as had been suggested to her, and then ventured to start out all alone.

Slowly she went down the lane into the main road, and when she had got about a quarter of a mile from the house, her feet "received strength," and she found that every step she took she could walk better. It was so very wonderful. When Ruth started, she had so much weakness and pain in her feet and ankles she could hardly walk at all, and now she felt that God had heard her prayers for strength that she might be able to get to the House of God that day. And not only so, but from that time, though still a cripple, yet for many years she was able to walk comparatively well. (Ruth later lived near Hastings, and often walked three or four miles to Mr. Hull's Chapel there.)

Thus Ruth was able to reach the Chapel, and it was so good to be there! especially after being helped by God in such a remarkable way. She stayed to dinner, and, after the afternoon service, started to walk home. When she got to the place where her feet "received strength," she stood still in amazement, and blessed and praised God for His great goodness to her. As she looked round on the fields and the trees, every little bird seemed to join with her in praising her great Creator; and even the flowers by the wayside, and the blades of grass, seemed to have new beauty; and in all of them was seen the handiwork of that great God Who, in His wonderful mercy and love, had given her strength. She truly realised the words you will find in the Prophecy of Isaiah, chapter lv., verse 12: "For ye shall go out with joy, and be led forth with peace: the mountains and the hills shall break forth before you into singing, and all the trees of the field shall clap their hands. Instead of the thorn shall come up the fir tree, and instead of the brier shall come up the myrtle tree: and it shall be to the LORD for a name, for an everlasting sign that shall not be cut off."

The family had finished their tea and had gone out when Ruth got back, and she was very glad to take a piece of bread and butter to eat, and to be alone, that she might enjoy the love and friendship of the Lord Jesus which she so sweetly felt. When it was time, she quickly put the children to bed, and then retired herself, with the blessed knowledge that God was her Friend and that she could truly say, "He hath done all things well!"

CHAPTER VIII

"PRAISE YE THE LORD!"

"It is a good thing to give thanks unto the Lord,
and to sing praises unto Thy Name, O Most High."
Psalm xcii. 1.

"When the Lord appears in view,
Old things pass, and all is new;
Love Divine o'erflows the soul,
Love does all their sins control."

IT was with something of this feeling that our young friend got up for her daily work the next morning, for nothing seemed to be any trouble to her; and besides, how wonderful it was to her that she could walk better! Even going down the stairs was quite different, and though she had black looks and cross words to bear, they did not matter. She could get the children and the breakfast ready more quickly; and after breakfast there was plenty to do. The milk pails had to be washed, and now she could step over the sill of the door, which before had been such a trouble to her. Perhaps you do not know what a door sill is, but in country houses it used to be very common, and you could easily be tripped up by it if you were not careful. Ruth carried the pails out to dry, which she had been unable to do, or only sometimes, and then with great difficulty. As soon as she got out of the door, and was putting them on a bench under the old yew tree, the Lord spoke these words to her heart: "He brought me up also out of an horrible pit, out of the miry clay, and set my feet upon a rock, and established my goings. And He hath put a new song in my mouth, even praise unto our God." She felt she must leap for joy at the Lord's goodness to her, and she sang the hymn:

> "All hail the power of Jesus' Name,
> Let angels prostrate fall;
> Bring forth the royal diadem,
> And crown Him Lord of all!"

And for some days after, when she was alone, she still kept on singing it. She could also say, "O that men would praise the Lord for His goodness, and for His wonderful works to the children of men."

I will only mention one more thing about Ruth, and then leave her for the present. The next time she was able to get to Chapel, Mr. Mockford took for his text: "Thine eyes shall see the King in His beauty: they shall behold the land that is very far off" (Isaiah xxxii. 17.). This was made a great blessing to her, and at the close of the service they sang the hymn, 247, which I have told you Ruth had written on the wall of her room:

> "O Lord, I would delight in Thee!"

This was almost more than she could bear, and as soon as she could she crept away down to the bottom of the Chapel graveyard; and there she told the Lord that she would try and delight herself in Him, for He was "her best, her only Friend." Like the Ruth we read of in the Bible, she felt she wanted to be with the Lord's people as long as she lived; also that she might be buried with them, just where she then stood, in the Heathfield burying ground.

Now my story is ended. You may be interested to know that Ruth is still living, and can say with the Psalmist: "I am a wonder unto many; but Thou art my strong Refuge." She is now an old lady, and has passed through many more trials and temptations, but her loving Friend, the Lord Jesus, has watched over her, preserved her, blessed her, and provided for all her needs; so that He

"Daily gives her cause to raise
New Ebenezers to His praise."

Dear children and young people, is this Friend your Friend? or is it your desire and prayer that He may be so? He has said, "Seek, and ye shall find;" and "Him that cometh to Me I will in no wise cast out." May the Holy Spirit place in your young hearts a deep need of the Saviour, that you may indeed "Seek the Lord while He may be found, and call upon Him while He is near;" and also give you the same love to the House of God as He did to Ruth, so that your prayer may be:

"Give *me*, O Lord, a place
Within Thy blest abode;
Among the children of Thy grace,
The servants of my God."

LITTLE BILL AT THE PUMP

PART I

THE pastor of Rossville church considered it both his privilege and his duty to superintend the Sunday-school connected with his own congregation. He always endeavoured to make it what, in his judgment, every Sunday-school should be; that is, the kind and faithful hand that should gather in from the paths of the destroyer, the outcast, the neglected and the friendless, and lead them to the fold of God. He frequently took long walks about the town to accomplish this important duty.

On one occasion, as he was passing to the house of prayer on a Sabbath morning, he discovered, near a public pump, a group of some half-dozen boys vigorously applying themselves to a game of marbles. He approached the spot where they were, without seeming to go out of his way, and thus came quite near them before they were aware of it; and in a pleasant tone addressed them.

"Good morning, boys. Is there any thing here by which a person can get a drink of water at this pump?"

Notwithstanding the gentleness of the salutation, they were all aroused at once, and showed no small surprise at my presence and unexpected question. Standing for a brief moment in silence, they suddenly wheeled and ran off at the top of their speed;—all, save one, who commenced a slow, backward step, desiring to get away, but to do so at the same time with a little more self-possession than his companions had exhibited.

The manner in which he eyed me while endeavouring to accomplish his retreat, and indeed his entire demeanour, pleased and interested me much, and deeply engaged my attention; and I felt impressed with the thought that a prize was before me.

He evidently wished, before leaving, to regain some marbles that, in the confusion of the flight of the other boys, had been left on the ground. I therefore gathered them up, and reaching them out to him, said –

"These, I think, fairly belong to you."

I then held up one, in particular, between my thumb and finger, and added,

"This one must be better than the rest. It is larger, and has several colours. What do you call it?"

Advancing, for the first time, a step towards me, he replied –

"Yes, that is the best; it is the king. I call it Napoleon; it is the very best of the bunch."

"It is certainly a fine one," I continued. "I like it much. When I was a boy I loved to play marbles. I had a little bag full of them."

"What! *you* used to play marbles?"

"Yes, when I was a boy I did; and I think, too, I have seen the day when I could pretty nigh beat you."

Drawing a step nearer to me, with a smile, a nod and a wink harmoniously combined, and a good deal of emphasis, he said –

"I tell you what, I can play pretty well; and you would have to throw first-rate to beat me. Why, I have won all these," (pulling out of his pocket a handful of marbles,) "and yesterday I sold twenty for six cents. Did *you* used to win many?"

"Oh, I never played to win."

"For what then?"

"For the fun of it."

"Well, I know there is fun in it; but I like to win. I suppose you do not play marbles now, because you are a man."

Finding myself on quite good terms with my new pupil, I thought it best to take another tack, and come a little closer to him. Said I –

"You seem to be rather a friendly little fellow, and I should like to know your name, where you live, and what you do for a living."

"My name is William; but people generally call me Bill. I live downtown, and I don't do much of anything but play marbles."

"I should like to see you often," said I.

"Well, as to that, I am here about every Sunday, unless when I go sailing."

"You must come and see me."

"Come and see *you!*"

"Yes, why not?"

"Oh, you don't want me to come and see you."

"Yes, I do, and I have some beautiful picture-books, which I will show you, and tell you all about them; and I have a large yard where you can play; and if you will come and see me, I will make you a present of something that will please you."

His countenance plainly disclosed the surprise with which he heard these things; and how really, too, his little mind was exercised between doubt and confidence. Rocking his body, first on one foot, then on the other, and casting a look thoughtfully around him for a moment, he calmly inquired –

"Where do you live?"

I informed him.

"Why, somebody told me that the minister lived there."

"So he does, and I am he."

"You the minister!"

"Yes."

"And you want me to come and see you?"

"Yes, indeed I do. Come, and then you will know if I am glad to see you."

"Well, I must come some time."

I then made an effort to bring him nearer still to the object I had in view from the beginning of our conversation. I inquired –

"Do you know where Rossville church is?"

"O yes, it is on Galloway Street."

"There is a Sunday-school in that church, and I am going to it. Will you go with me?"

"I go with you to the Sunday-school! Oh, I cannot go now."

And he cast a careful glance over his person, evidently impressed with a sense of shame at his dirty and ragged condition.

"Why not go now?"

"Oh, I never went to Sunday-school in my life; and I cannot go now, anyhow."

"Do not say you cannot. You can. Come with me. I will take care of you."

"I am too dirty and ragged, it will not do;"—taking, at the same time, a still narrower look at his hands; and then pulling the fag-ends of a rent in his trousers over his naked limb.

"Never mind—just stop here. I will pump the water, and you can wash your hands and face, and that will do."

"You, sir?! pump water for me, to wash!?", he cried, quite astounded at the very idea.

"Yes, certainly I will."

Again he hesitated; but finally said –

"Well, I will;" and at once laid off an old half-brimmed hat from his head, made bare his arms, and by our united labours, there were soon presented a clean face and a clean pair of hands.

I took from my pocket a white handkerchief, and shaking out its folds, presented it to him, saying:

"Take this, and wipe your face and hands with it"

"Oh, no! it is so white—no, not with that."

"Yes, yes, with this; I do so sometimes when I am out of doors and want to wash, and can get nothing else to wipe with—it will not hurt it."

He complied; and on returning the handkerchief, asked, with a tone and manner that could not be misunderstood,

"Do you like me?"

The question went to my very heart. I knew what feeling prompted it; I knew its import, and felt its force.

"Yes, I like you much. I hope you like me."

"Well, – I think I do."

"Come," I added, "now let us go to the Sunday-school. We shall be late."

"Do you think I had better go now?"

"By all means. I want you to hear the little girls and boys at school sing, and then you can see the books and pictures;—and, above all, if you will go often enough, you can learn to read yourself."

"I cannot read much, I know; but I can sing, and whistle, and play the Jew's harp."

I took his hand, and we passed on towards the church. On coming to the door, I said –

"This is the place. When we go in, you will see the school, and the scholars will all be glad to see you with them." Looking me full in the face, he said, with much earnestness –

"Oh, sir, I cannot go in—I cannot. Do let me go back, do. I am not well dressed, and I know the fellows in the room there will laugh and make fun of me."

"They will not—they shall not—you may depend on me."

His little chin quivered and his entire frame trembled. He stood an instant in thoughtful silence; (my own heart breathed the silent prayer to Heaven, that his courage might not fail him;) and then seizing my hand with both of his, he exclaimed –

"I will go in; you will take care of me."

I have no power to describe fully the thrilling emotions of that moment. I then knew "I had my man;" for he confided in me—he loved me. I had won his soul—his whole soul.

We passed in, hand in hand. The scholars understood my intent, and knew how to behave toward the new-comer. There was no strange or bold gazing upon the ragged boy.

We took our seats together. After sitting a little while, I arose, and stated that now we would open the school.

Everything that was done seemed much to interest the lad. He was supplied with cards containing lessons and pictures, while several things were explained to him. He appeared to be rapt in wonder. Surprise and joy mingled in his looks, and he seemed to say to himself—"This is all new to me! I have never seen the like before!"

On closing the exercises of the school, he was committed to the special care of a worthy and skillful person, and at once a mutual attachment was formed between them. This individual proposed to the boy to go home with him, and thus become more acquainted with him and his family.

"No," said he, "not to-day. I will go home alone, and tell my mother about the minister and the school; and tomorrow I shall be glad to have you come and see us."

A just and honest self-respect led him to desire first to see his mother, that she might make preparation to appear to the best advantage in her power before his benefactors; and further, it showed clearly, as it subsequently proved, that in that then young and untutored mind lay the germs of a true ambition, and a correct discernment of duty.

The visit was made the next day according to the request. The boy's father and mother were both addicted to the excessive use of intoxicating liquors. The former, however, followed the seas, and was but little with his family, and that only at long intervals and for periods of short duration. He was at this time absent.

The wretched mother was deeply affected at the kindness her boy had received from strangers; and seemed scarcely able to account for it.

The Sunday after his first visit to the school, Bill appeared in his new suit, obtained for him by his good and faithful patron, to whose care he had been transferred.

No better scholar, as to behaviour, punctuality and application, was found in that, or any other school, than this same little Bill.

His brothers and sisters, (the latter were older than himself,) influenced by his example, were induced to attend the school with him, and his mother was persuaded to attend church. Nor was this young disciple satisfied until, with the aid of his teacher, he had won over to the school and to attendance at church, several other vagrant children, among whom were nearly, if not all the boys who, at our first interview, ran away from the pump!

The pastor finally left this field of his successful labours; and for a long time had no further opportunity to know the history of Little Bill.

PART II

IN the year 1839, the same pastor had occasion to visit what was then called the "Far West." At the close of a beautiful day in the month of July, just at dusk, as he was walking along one of the streets of a Western city of much note, with one arm thrown backward across his back, he felt the sudden and firm grasp of some other hand upon his own as it was thus placed. Turning quickly about, he found himself facing a young and well-dressed gentleman, of tall and elegant stature, and in all respects exceedingly fair to look upon. At the same time he manifested very deep emotion, for which the pastor was utterly unable to account. Without loosing his hold, the stranger said,

"You do not know me!"

"No, yet I see about your countenance something that is quite familiar to me. Have we ever met before? And, if so, when and where?"

The young man became more and more agitated, while large tears started to his eyes, and fell rapidly down his cheeks; but he uttered not a word.

"Tell me," said I, "do tell me what this means. You distress me."

"Do you remember little Bill that you found at the pump in Rossville,– the one you led to the Sunday-school, and used to love so well? I am he."

And throwing his arms about my neck, he wept like a babe. I need not say, that he did not weep alone.

"Ah," he continued, "that interview with you at the pump was the moment of my salvation. You, as the instrument in the hands of Divine Providence, saved me. Ever since our last separation, I have longed to see you. You have shared most sincerely in my supplications at the throne of grace. You passed the store yonder, where I was; and at the first glance I knew you, and followed you, almost without any thought of what I was doing, and seized that very hand which once, when I was a poor, outcast boy, led me to the house of God! Your singular and unfailing kindness to me at that time has been in my thoughts by day, and often in my dreams at night. Then, I knew not the spirit that prompted your actions; but now, I trust I do. It was the spirit of compassion that flows from the gospel; the spirit of Him who went about doing good."

"I am thankful," said the pastor, "thus to meet you, and especially to find that you are so deeply and truly impressed with those good and holy things which at that time it was my earnest desire and effort to fix, lastingly, in your mind. I too can say that you have shared in my prayers to our great Creator and Redeemer, from the time of our first acquaintance to this hour. I hope you have done and still are doing well in things temporal as well as in things spiritual."

"As to what you early taught me," he remarked, "you must have been quite successful, certainly so far as impressions and my own understanding of them are concerned; for, indeed, it seems to me that not even then, when I was but a child and so very ignorant, did you utter one word of instruction or counsel to me that I have not always clearly and definitely retained in my mind. Why, sir, I can remember them all now, even as if they had been imparted to me but yesterday.

"All that I am," he seriously added, "I owe under God to you; and not only myself, but others of our family may express the same, for it is equally true of them."

"I should be very happy," said I, "to know something about your parents and brothers and sisters."

"About my poor father," he replied, with much emotion, "I can say but little that is definite, as he was much abroad, and finally, some years since, died from home. But I remember to have seen him when I thought he was really serious, and even affected to tears at beholding the change for the better, which he could not but discover in his family; and I am quite sure that my mother (especially after she commenced attending church) used to talk with him about his duty to God and us.

"I recollect distinctly his once saying to me, after hearing me recite my Sunday-school lesson to my oldest sister, 'My son, I beg you never to be tired of your Sunday-school. The people there are your friends. I hope you will continue to be a good boy, and grow up to be a good and useful man.'

"This address affected me to tears; and on my father's perceiving it, he arose, came to me, and putting his hand on my head, said,—'God bless you, my son,'—and then passed by out of doors. I am not mistaken, I think, that he wept as he went. I cannot but indulge the hope that in his heart he garnered up the good seed, and at the hour of his death may have found pardon and favour from Heaven.

"My mother became a true penitent, and a humble follower of the Saviour, and died in great peace. I have rarely seen a death more triumphant and happy.

"My brothers and sisters, as you doubtless will recollect, were enticed to the Sunday-school, which early brought them happily and effectually under religious influence, that was not lost upon them. They have all grown up pious men and women, and maintain exemplary Christian lives.

"Our Heavenly Father has favoured me with more than a mere competency of this world's goods. He has also given me an honourable place and name in His Church, and blessed me with the privilege of being a Sunday-school teacher.

"And now," continued my young friend, "you must go with me; for I must see you at my home." It was with sincere regret that I was compelled, owing to previous engagements which I could not set aside, to forego his pleasure.

"Well," said he, "I have one more favour to ask of you."

"What is that?" I inquired.

"That you would raise your hat and permit me to cut from your head a single lock of your hair. You will not deny me this?"

"No, I will not."

Taking from his pocket a pair of merchant's scissors, he accomplished his wish.

"Now," said I, "allow me to receive from you the same memorial."—And there we stood under the open sky, exchanging that common reminder of love and friendship,—there we stood together, for the first time after the lapse of several years, in which interval the young minister had passed to middle life, and the boy to manhood,—there we were together for the last time, until we stand, as I trust we finally shall, before "the throne of God and the Lamb," in "glory everlasting."

My friend Bill has now passed on to heaven, and hope that we may be yet able to give all the particulars of the event; which would supply us with another instructive and profitable little volume. He died happy, knowing in Whom he had believed. In the cause of Christ he faithfully laboured all the days of his pious pilgrimage, and in aid of it he contributed cheerfully and liberally of his monetary substance according to his honest ability.

No one branch of religious duty was dearer to him, or more engaged his attention, and in none did he serve with more affection, ardour and success, than in that of the Sunday-school, for he knew its benefits and blessedness by his own happy experience.

In vain should I attempt to give a full and just description of my own joyous feelings in connection with this occasion. Tongue and pen would fail me in the effort. But, thanks be to God then and now (and I trust it will continue so with me until this present life shall terminate,) this entire circumstance, in all its aspects and bearings, opens to me a fountain of sweet and cheering peace. It is the peace that flows only out of the deep conviction "that he which converteth a sinner from the error of his way shall save a soul from death and hide a multitude of sins."

"Not unto us, O Lord, not unto us, but unto Thy Name give glory, for Thy mercy and Thy truth's sake."

Reader, cast thy bread upon the waters, for thou shalt find it after many days.

SEQUEL OF
"LITTLE BILL AT THE PUMP"

PART III

HAVING occasion to visit again the "Far West," and feeling a strong desire to learn more of the active life and closing days of "Little Bill at the Pump," I turned considerably out of my direct route, to the city where had passed most of his life, and near which still resided his widow.

On an evening in August, 1871, I found myself a guest for the night at a hotel in that city. The landlord had known Bill as "Willie", and spoke of him as an active man of business, a large-hearted Christian, universally respected and beloved. From him, also, I ascertained the residence of Bill's widow. Thither, the next morning, I hastened.

On being admitted by the servant, I inquired for the lady of the house, and was informed that she was confined to her room by sickness, and could receive no one.

Personally, we were strangers, having never met. I sent my card, thinking it probable that she had heard of me from her husband. Quickly the word came for me to come to her chamber. On my entering where she lay bolstered up as an invalid, she instantly extended both of her hands, and, taking, mine, exclaimed, –

"Do we meet at last? God be thanked! It is more than I ever expected. You are my precious husband's loved and honoured protector and counsellor, of whom he has talked so often and much to me."

Her eyes were full, and so were mine.

"How kind of you," she continued, "to come thus far to see me! I am glad – thrice glad! You know not how deeply Willie loved you. He always spoke of you as 'my own dear minister,' 'my best earthly friend.'"

"Willie was very dear to me," I replied. "He seemed so very anxious, when but a child, to do and say as I did, it made me the more careful to always set him a good example."

"Yes," she rejoined: "he copied all he could remember of your example through life."

"Have you been long sick?" I asked.

"I was never strong; but since I buried Willie I have considerably run down. It has left me very sad. But all this is with my Divine Father, with whose will I am content. Physically, I seem to be wasting away; but my hope above is constantly strengthened, so that I am not disturbed by thoughts of death."

It was most refreshing to hear her converse, so calm was she, so consistent, so pious and full of faith.

"Have you no family?" I inquired.

"Two lovely children were given to us,—a son and a daughter. But they were removed at an early age,—one two and the other four. They were scarcely divided in death, dying on the same day, and almost at the same hour, with croup. They sleep in one grave. Willie was with me then, and we met the blow together.

"The son," she added, "bore *your* name; the daughter, that of the kind lady, Ann Franklin, to whose care Willie by you was transferred. You see how profound was his esteem and grateful his memory of you both."

Communicating to her my wishes in regard to obtaining further information respecting the life and last days of her late husband, she replied, –

"I shall be happy in forwarding your desire. My husband left a diary; but, in looking it over since his death, I find this note:—'Allow no public use to be made of this diary.'

"I must heed that," she remarked. "I can, however, relate much to you."

"I shall remain at least a day or two," I said, "and shall have an opportunity to see you more, and to examine these items and sketches."

Such was the arrangement; and, as the result, I am able to give the following.

Willie was employed as errand-boy in a store of his native town, where his good behaviour, activity and strict honesty gave him great favour with his employer.

The bookkeeper of the establishment (a noble, generous and educated young man) noticed the boy's conduct, and became very warmly attached to him. Among other things which he taught him was *keeping accounts*, in which he became quite expert.

At the age of eighteen, Willie emigrated to the West; and, with the excellent letters which were given him from high sources, certifying to his moral worth and mercantile abilities, he found no difficulty in obtaining a place in an extensive dry-goods store in the city of Denver.

The principal was a middle-aged gentleman, of but few words, but a very close observer of all that transpired around him.

The new clerk's whole tenor of conduct, in the store and elsewhere, being entirely unexceptionable, made so favourable an impression that soon was committed to him the oversight of most of the responsible branches of the concern.

He was a rare salesman, endowed with commanding grace of manners, as attractive as accommodating.

He united himself with the church of his denomination, and was a punctual attendant; he was a devoted teacher in Sunday-school; and, gifted as he was in both thought and language, he was soon distinguished as a Christian of influence in religious circles as well as in the community at large.

His employer had but one child, a daughter, who, at the time of the young clerk's introduction to the family, was scarcely seventeen.

These two persons were forming a mutual attachment, apparently without being conscious of it. With Willie, however, the emotion of pure affection increased rapidly, until it disturbed him. He was without family distinction, and penniless, while the young lady was the only child of a well-to-do merchant and of no small weight of character in society.

But he must be honourable and just: therefore it seemed to him prudent, and, indeed, a matter of duty, to withdraw from his present post, that he might no longer nourish this strong attachment.

Accordingly, without rendering any reason, he surprised his employer by informing him that he was about to abandon his place.

"What!" exclaimed the merchant; "what is the matter? Do you dislike your position? I thought you were satisfied. If your compensation is not sufficient, I will increase it."

"I am not dissatisfied. You have been generous and kind to me," said the young man. "But there are circumstances which, I think, justify my intended withdrawal."

"What can they be? Allow me to inquire," said the merchant.

The clerk was wordless.

"Ah! perhaps I have it," interrupted the interrogator. "You are now nearly or quite in your majority, and you desire to occupy a larger field,— one which has a partner's share. Well, I have thought of that. If you consent, I shall forthwith consider you as my partner in business."

The young man was much surprised, exclaiming, "Why, my dear sir, I have no capital! I have not five hundred dollars in the world."

"I am aware of that," was the reply. "It is not money I want of you, but your time, talent, honesty, and above all, your example and influence. These you have; and I ask for them. My young friend," continued the merchant, "I will speak frankly. I fully know and appreciate your character. It is above money. But of the latter, even, I mean that you shall have enough yet. Such is my design. What say you?"

The young man remained silent, not knowing what to say.

"Ah, Willie, Willie, I see it all," continued the merchant. "You love my daughter; and, let me tell you, she reciprocates that love. I have known this for some time. My wife and myself have talked it over. Her parents will not object. You twain can arrange for a co-partnership in your own way, if you choose."

This settled the matter with the Willie. He hastened to the object of his love, and, expressing to her his ardent and sincere affection, proffered her his hand as her future husband.

The young lady replied, "We will leave that to my parents."

They were soon after united in holy wedlock.

Willie remained in the family, and in trade with his wife's father, until the death of the latter; and he carried on the store afterwards, till he himself was removed from time; and now it is the property of James Archer, long his bosom friend, and for a few years last past his business partner.

"The history of James is a little remarkable," said the widow; "and it is so closely connected with Willie's as to be interesting.

"I can state it briefly, so that you will get the substance.

"My husband was passing from dinner to his store, when he observed on an open lot several boys in a circle around some object. Coming up, he saw two lads on the ground, in a desperate struggle, who were no more than thirteen or fourteen years of age.

"'What is all this?' cried Willie.

"The urchins, discovering a man present, scattered forthwith. The two in combat arose from the ground, and as the under one regained his feet, doubling up his fist and thrusting it into the face of the other, he said, with an oath, 'Jim, I will whip you yet,' and turned after the other boys.

"Poor Jim burst into tears, saying, 'I didn't want to fight; but I couldn't help it.'

"'My little man, how did it happen?' asked Willie, in a kind voice.

"'Why, you see, Bob Sanders struck my brother on the side of his head, and knocked him over. I told him not to strike my little brother,— when he turned and kicked me right hard.

"'The boys shouted, "A ring! make a ring and let them fight it out!" I said I didn't want to fight. "Coward! coward!" they cried. Then Bob struck me in the face. You see how it is bruised. I clinched him, and threw him flat on his back. He came pretty nigh turning me under, though, when some boy said, "Throat him, Jim! throat him!" I did grip his throat with all my might, till you came up.'

"'You have whipped him, then?'

"'Well, perhaps I did while I had him down and by the throat. But he is bigger and older than me, and I reckon he will pound me awfully, some time. And when I go home now, mother, I know, will thrash me; and so I shall get it both ways.'

"'Where does your mother live?'

"'Just around that old grocery on the corner there,' (pointing to it.)

"'Well, I am going that way, and I will stop in with you and tell your mother what I know about the matter.'

"'Will you speak on my side?' asked the boy.

"'I will certainly state that I think you were abused, and were only defending your brother and yourself.'

"'That will do: it is just so; and, as you saw part of it, I think mother will believe both of us together, and she won't whip me.'

"So (like Bill and his friend at the pump) the two passed on to the house near the grocery. They found the mother in quite a state of alarm, as the younger brother had hastened home from the fight and told her that Bob Sanders was killing Jim for taking his part.

"On the facts being stated, the mother was entirely satisfied, and so was Jim.

"My husband had no more than reached the store, when Jim appeared, and, removing his cap, said, 'Mr. Taylor, I have come to thank you for your kindness to me today, and for what you said to mother. I did not think of it till you were gone, and so I thought I would stop in and tell you.'

"'You are very thoughtful," said Mr. Taylor; 'and I am glad that it so happened that I could speak for you.'

"'Yes: you have been right kind; and I want to know what I can do for you.'

"'What would you like to do?' inquired Mr. Taylor.

"'I would like to come here and sweep the store and do chores about.'

"The old merchant, hearing this, said to his son-in-law, 'Willie, that is a nice boy. Take him, if you like, and tell him he shall have pay if he behaves well.'

"And so James was installed chore-boy of the store.

"'Well, my lad,' continued Mr. Taylor, 'who knows but what you may yet be a wealthy merchant? Such things sometimes happen. But I have a proposition of another kind to make to you.'

"'What is it?' asked the boy.

"'You shall know tomorrow,' he was told.

"'I shall indeed be glad to do anything for you, Mr. Taylor.'

"He then bounded home like a fawn, and communicated the wonderful news to his mother, who remarked that she thought she saw something good in the gentleman's face.

"'When are you to go there?'

"'Now – right away, mother.'

"So the next day, after Jim had worked a little and become slightly acquainted with his new duties, Mr. Taylor, calling him into the counting-room said, 'Well, James, do you think you will like to stay here?'

"'Oh, yes; I know I shall.'

"'Do you go to Sunday-school?'

"'No, sir,—not now. I did a while ago.'

"'Why did you leave off?'

"'Why, you see, the man who managed it didn't seem to care at all about me; and my teacher was downright mopish. So I quit.'

"'In my school,' said Mr. Taylor, 'I take care of my boys. Will you go with me?'

"'Yes, indeed; and I will go all the time, get my lessons, and try to be good.'

"'Now, James, I have another matter.'

"'What is that?' he asked.

"'You must see Bob Sanders, and settle your quarrel without a fight.'

"'Oh, sir, should I go there, he would pitch into me and thrash me like blazes.'

"'But I will go with you, and he shall not do that,' added Mr. Taylor.

"'I will go, then. But when?'

"'This afternoon,' he was told.

"'You won't let him beat me?'

"'No. Have no fears.'

"When they reached Bob's house, he was seated on the door-step alone, the rest of the family being absent. Seeing Jim with the man who had spoiled the fight, he seemed to imagine that it was still to come off. He arose, drew himself up at full height, and asked, 'Well, what's wanted?'

"'We have called, Robert, in a friendly way, to settle the unhappy difference between you and James, so that you will hereafter be friends,' replied Mr. Taylor.

"'Jim and I generally get along together pretty well; but I can't settle this without a fight. The boys say he has whipped me; and I won't stand that.'

"'But James says you are more than his match, and that he does not wish to fight you at all. Drop this, now, and be friends. I have rather a liking for you, Robert; and I am sure if you will take my advice it will be to your advantage. Come now; shake hands, and end this affair.'

"James at once offered his hand; but the other hesitated.

"'What makes you anxious about this, Mr. Taylor?' asked Bob.

"'For more reasons than one. James is now our chore-boy at the store, and he must not quarrel or fight. Then he is to help me in the Sunday-school.'

"'Sunday-school!' replied Bob. 'I went just one Sunday, and that will do for me all my lifetime.'

"'But it was not my school,' said Mr. Taylor.

"'No. Where's your school?'

"He was told.

"'And so Jim has got into the store, and is going to the Sunday-school? That is pretty well, I think.'

"'Robert,' said Mr. Taylor, 'you do not know how much I wish you and James to be at peace. When this takes place, I have something to propose to you that may affect your whole future life.'

"'I don't feel mad at Jim,' he said; 'and I think it was wrong that I struck his brother and him. But now the boys twit me that I have been whipped by one smaller and younger than me. I tell you what, that won't do.'

"'But,' replied Mr. Taylor, 'if they see you and James friendly, they will know the matter is over. Just shake hands, now, and let the past be forgotten.'

"Bob looked vaguely around in silence, then said, 'Well, let it all drop,' giving his hand to Jim.

"'Nobly done!' exclaimed Mr. Taylor; 'nobly done!

"'Now for my plan. You are both acquainted with the boys who were at that fight. I want to get them all into the Sunday-school. Robert, will you help?'

"'What! Go to Sunday-school?'

"'Yes,' answered Mr. Taylor.

"'I have no liking for that.'

"'Try it,' said Mr. Taylor; 'try it; and if you do not like it I will say no more.'

"'That is fair,' replied Bob, 'anyhow. When do you want me to begin?'

"'Next Sunday .'

"'Jim, will you go with me?'

"'O, I am going, anyhow,' he answered.

"'Well, I will join you, Mr. Taylor. What must we bring with us?'

"'Nothing. Just come to the school.'

"It was pleasant and lovely to see those boys turning to each other so kindly.

"The next Sunday morning found the two promptly at the school-room, when Mr. Taylor introduced them to the scholars as his *young friends*.

"Robert never left that school till called elsewhere. James continued, and is now its superintendent, taking the place of dear Willie.

"A maternal uncle, a sea-captain, wrote for his nephew Robert to come to him. He would give him a place in his ship, and when competent he should have the command. He went, and became a skilful and distinguished navigator, a pious officer, whose vessel was a floating Bethel. He often said that his Sabbath-school training was the means of his salvation and the cause of his usefulness to others.

"James proved so highly trustworthy that in a short time he was promoted to salesman, then to chief accountant; and when the senior partner died he was admitted junior member of the firm.

"No two could ever be more sincerely united in friendship than Willie and James. The latter was strictly the pupil of the former in business as well as religion.

"In Willie's last sickness—which was a quick consumption, brought on nobody knew how—James was constantly with him. A few hours before his death, they held a conversation of considerable length, when the dying man implored his Christian brother never to cease gathering into the Sunday-school the reckless children of the streets. 'It is the Lord's net,' said he,—'the school: be careful always to cast it on the right side, and it shall come up full.'

"At the conclusion of this conversation, his end being very nigh, he said, '*Let death alone part us.*' And, with one hand clasped in the hand of his friend and the other in the hand of his wife, he passed away with a sweet smile upon his serene and Heaven-lighted countenance."

Burying her face in her hands, the dear woman wept long and bitterly, but silently.

Recovering herself, she asked, "Did you observe a beautiful residence on the right as you came from the city?"

"Yes: I noticed it particularly," I replied.

"That is James's house,—a charming place indeed, with inmates as intelligent and lovely as the house is elegant and attractive. The family are away now, on a journey East. James will regret missing you. Your name is familiar to him. He has so frequently heard it that it has real being in his memory.

"So, you see, the good influence imparted by you in the first case is active and passing on still; and, as James has been perhaps more successful than his immediate predecessor in 'taming wild boys' (as Willie used to express it), he will have many to represent him when his pilgrimage is over, and so on, from one generation to another, like an ever-flowing stream, to the end of the world.

"How interesting and sublime the thought that works done for God and humanity never die! The doers must cease, but the deeds themselves are eternal: they have a record on high."

"You are weary, my friend," I said. "Rest now."

"Yes," she replied. "But I may add a request that you will step into the parlour and see with what care and taste your *convert boy* has in keeping your photograph.

"And you remember the lock of hair?" (showing a costly locket, which she constantly wore about her person.) "Here is your hair, with Willie's and mine.

"'Take this, Lizzie,' said he to me in his last sickness, 'and wear it for my sake, and for his who has been more to me than a father.'

"And now," she said, "we part. May God bless and keep you evermore! We shall meet again, and Willie will be with us."

One thing more remains to be stated. It is my visit to the burying-ground. There can be seen a neat marble shaft, with the inscription beginning –

"SACRED TO THE MEMORY OF
WILLIE TAYLOR.
HE WAS A JUST MAN, FULL OF FAITH AND
GOOD WORKS."

My impressions and reflections I shall not attempt to describe. They were emotions of joy and hope and gratitude to my Redeemer for the blessing bestowed upon the youthful labours of His servant, the good fruit of His grace, to the honour of His own great Name.

THE END

WHO IS A COWARD?

THE CHALLENGE

"My son," said Alfred's father, as he was accompanying his son to school for the first time, "My son, if sinners entice thee, consent thou not. I have been to school before you, and I know that many temptations will beset you, of which you have hitherto had little experience. This has led me to hesitate long before I could bring my mind to trusting you so far away, and for so long a time, from your home. Nor should I venture to do so now, but for my confidence in the gentleman who will take charge of you.

"But, after all, much will depend on yourself. Your conscience will be your monitor, if you will but regard it; and the word of God will be your sure guide, if you will but consult it. 'Wherewithal shall a young man cleanse his way? by taking heed thereto according to thy word.'

"I will tell you," he continued, "a few of the trials and temptations I had to endure when I was a schoolboy. Perhaps my experience may be useful to you.

"I had been taught from a child, as you have been, to reverence the Bible, to read it daily, and to kneel, morning and evening, by my bedside, to pray; and I never once thought of forsaking at school the good practices which I had followed at home. But I found it a hard matter to keep them up. I was laughed at by my bed-room companions, and was soon nicknamed through the school as 'the little Deacon.' Mischievous tricks were played upon me; and I was so often interrupted, that I thought I *must* give up praying to God, and reading His word.

"But, happily, I remembered these words, 'My son, keep thy father's commandment, and forsake not the law of thy mother; bind them continually upon thine heart, and tie them about thy neck. When thou goest, it shall lead thee; and when thou sleepest, it shall keep thee; and when thou awakest, it shall talk with thee;' and I was thus encouraged to persevere. It was not long before I was let alone; some of my schoolfellows took courage to follow my example, and those who did not, respected the practice which they would not imitate.

"Another of my temptations was to join in forbidden sports, or mischievous tricks. I was frequently at first, invited to do so; but when these invitations were found to be unavailing, I was no longer troubled with them; and all the harm that came to me from my refusals was a nickname or two, which happily, did not disturb my peace.

"But there was one trial to which I was exposed, to which I too much yielded. By copying the example of other boys, I became less guarded against the employment of foolish words and phrases; and occasionally found myself using even very improper language. I did not duly reflect upon the Scripture, 'That every idle word that men shall speak, they shall give account thereof in the day of judgment.'

"Many times, when I first began to acquire this habit, I checked myself, and was very unhappy to think how nearly I had offended; but still the habit gained upon me, and I no longer felt so troubled at the recollection of what I had said. It was many years after I left school, that I was quite enabled to leave off the use of words that, at best, were unmeaning; and too many of which were sinful.

"I do not think," continued Alfred's father, "that you will have so much in the way of bad example and ridicule to tempt and try you as I had; but I believe that boys have still wicked natures and inclinations, just as they ever had—you, Alfred, as well as others; and that no care, nor the best instruction, can prevent much evil where many meet together.

"My earnest and last advice to you, therefore, is, to seek the help of your heavenly Father, Who is always near you; to read His word, though you may be taunted for it; to do what you know to be right, and avoid what your heart tells you is wrong, just as though your parents were present; to form no friendships with boys who make light of serious things; and especially to watch over your thoughts and words with strict care. Remember the words of the Lord Jesus Christ, 'I say unto you, Swear not at all; neither by heaven; for it is God's throne: nor by the earth; for it is His footstool. —But let your communication be, Yea, yea; Nay, nay: for whatsoever is more than these cometh of evil.'"

You need not think that Alfred was tired with hearing his father's good counsel; for indeed he was not. He knew that it was intended for his benefit; and he was thankful for his father for putting him once more in mind of what had often been told him. He resolved to treasure his father's words in his heart, and to obey them too. And it is almost certain that he then secretly prayed to God that he might have strength given him to walk in the ways of true piety and peace.

Do you ask why this is so very likely? It is because Alfred really loved to pray at all times; and this was a very fit time for secret prayer. And we shall see, also, that he was preserved from the very sin against which his father cautioned him, although his firmness exposed him to scorn: and surely he would on some occasions, at least, have given way if he had not sought and obtained help from God for the time of need.

Alfred soon became happy at school; the more so in finding that he could read his Bible, and kneel by his bedside, without any interruption from his schoolfellows. Some of them made a practice of doing it too; and though it is to be feared, from the hurried manner in which they went through this duty, and the foolish talking which immediately followed, that they thought but little of prayer, except as a form; yet, Alfred—with whom it was not a mere form—could enjoy his own thoughts, and resign himself calmly to sleep at night, or rise freshly to the duties of the day, with the happy consciousness that he had committed himself to the kind keeping of the great God his Saviour.

There was one boy in the school with whom Alfred soon formed a sort of boyish friendship. His name was Herbert. There were many things in the circumstances of these two boys that were alike. Both of them were sons of pious parents; they had been brought up to the same kind of habits at their homes; they had learned the same hymns in their childhood; they were both very fond of singing, and each was pleased to find that the other could sing the same tunes to the same hymns; the books they had brought with them to school were just such as each knew his own parent would approve; and, in short, they were well pleased with each other. They also slept in the same room, and when they sometimes lay awake for a short time, they talked together about their homes, and the ways of home, or sometimes about the different histories they had read in the Bible.

And yet, for all these points of resemblance, there was one important particular in which they very much differed. Herbert was irresolute. He, like Alfred, had formed many good plans as to what he would do, and what he would not do, when he was at school; but these plans were not laid in dependence on any strength but his own: no wonder, therefore, that he was often led astray. Besides this, Herbert was fond of being noticed and admired by his companions, so that he was often induced to go further in acts of daring adventure than he knew to be quite right. Just in proportion, too, to his love of admiration, was his sensitiveness when any slight was shown him. A smile of derision, or a word of reproach, or even the fancy that he was thought of little account, often made him more unhappy than when he had really done wrong.

Among the schoolfellows of Herbert and Alfred were two or three boys who were not infrequently guilty of using profane language, and taking the name of God in vain. This awful practice they carefully concealed from their master; but when they were by themselves they gave way to it, and appeared to take delight in it. They foolishly thought that it was manly to cast off the fear of God, and defy Him by their guilty language. They rolled their iniquity, as a sweet morsel, under their tongues. Unhappily, they found others of their companions who began to imitate them at first, and then to compete with them, and even to excel them in this particular sin.

It may seem strange, but it is not the less true, that, in the course of a few weeks, the language of the play-ground (when no master or usher was near) became fearfully wicked. The names of God, of the Divine Redeemer, of heaven, and of hell, became common words, and were mixed up with the most trifling affairs. The dreadful practice spread like wildfire. Boys, who but a short month before would have feared an oath, became vile blasphemers.

And yet so privately did the guilty habit gain ground, and so careful were the boys not to be overheard by their master, that it was long before the painful truth came to his knowledge. When it did, he lost no time, and spared no trouble to root out the mischief, and to awaken the consciences of his pupils to the enormity of their sin.

Herbert, no less than Alfred, had been brought up to reverence holy names and holy things; and he was shocked, very much shocked, when he first heard the utterance of an oath by a play-fellow. It would have been well for him if he had copied Alfred's example, and at once separated from all who so willfully broke the law of their God. But this he did not do. He thought it enough to set a guard upon his own lips—a guard, alas! too soon broken through. So true is it that—

> "Vice is a monster of such hideous mien,
>   As to be hated needs but to be seen;
> But, seen too oft, familiar grows her face:
> We first endure, then pity, then embrace."

One day, a few of the older boys of the school were sitting upon the playground bench, and among them was Herbert. What they were talking about is of little consequence; but, whatever it might be, their conversation was unhappily polluted by profaneness. It happened that Alfred passed by, and heard something that was said. He started, and looked up. Surely he must have been deceived. Alas! no. It was Herbert—his friend Herbert—whose voice he had heard taking the name of God in vain. Surprised and grieved, he went up to his friend, and began to remonstrate with him; but he was met with a shout of derision.

"Herbert is a good fellow," said one of the tempters; "he is none of your cowards and sneaks."

"Nor am I a coward or a sneak," replied Alfred; "but I must say that I should be very sorry."

"There, I said so," said the other, interrupting him; "I knew you would sneak."

"I do not know what you mean," was the reply.

The boy-bravo uttered a very profane expression. "There match that, if you can; and then we shall know whether you are a coward."

"I *am* a coward," said Alfred, meekly and sadly; "if that is the test, I am indeed a coward. I should be afraid to say what you have said," and he walked away, sorrowing that he should have witnessed such hardness of heart in his schoolfellows, and especially grieving for his friend Herbert. Again, a shout of mockery was raised against him, but it did not move him; and if afterwards he was seen with red and swollen eyes, he had not been crying about the scorn he had incurred, but for the sins of his companions. He knew the meaning of these words, "Rivers of waters run down mine eyes, because they keep not Thy law." (Psalm cxix. 136.)

Herbert was half inclined to retreat with Alfred. He knew that he ought to do so; but he hesitated; he was ashamed; he dreaded the derision of fools; he was afraid of being called a coward. That moment's hesitation riveted the claims of sin fast upon him. His hesitation was perceived by the profane boy who headed the set. "What, are you turning tail too?" he asked derisively. "You are not afraid, are you?"

"No, n–o," Herbert answered.

"Then"—but why should we write more? Herbert dreaded the scoffs of fellow-sinners more than the anger of God. From thenceforth he avoided the society of his friend Alfred, and was reckoned a hearty good fellow by the brave hearts in the school that could set their Maker at defiance. He had taken his first step in deliberate sin to prove that he was no coward; but it was not his last. In the next chapter we shall meet with him again.

"I believe I have had enough, replied poor Herbert.

CHAPTER II

THE FALL

HERBERT left school with a blemished character, or rather, with a mottled character. There were many things in which he had given satisfaction to his best friends, and there was much, also, that had endeared him to his school-fellows; but, on the other hand, he had in many respects disappointed the hopes which had been formed of him. The good impressions of his childhood had become faint, and his more amiable qualities had been obscured. One foolish, criminal weakness was at the root of the mischief—he could not bear to be singular; he had not the true courage to say "No," to any project or action which his conscience disapproved. He chose rather to "follow a multitude to do evil," than to walk alone in the plain and narrow path of rectitude.

Herbert was placed in the counting-house of a city merchant, in which were several clerks older than himself, though all were young men.

"Will you go with us tonight, Herbert?" asked one of these, a few weeks after he had joined their society. "A capital new piece is coming out at the Holliday Theatre."

"No, I think not," replied Herbert.

"Why, do you never mean to go to the theatre?"

97

"I do not know—perhaps I may—I had rather not go tonight."

"Ah, I see how it is," said his fellow-clerk, with a smile; "you are one of old Thompson's crew. I should not wonder if you were going off to some sermonizing. Mind you bring home the text," he continued with a smile of disdain.

Old Thompson, as he was sneeringly called, was one of the youngest of the clerks; but, like Herbert's old school-fellow Alfred, he had stood firm against the temptations with which he was surrounded.

> "His loyalty he kept, his love, his zeal;
> Nor numbers nor example with him wrought,
> To swerve from truth, or change his constant mind,
> Though single"—

Ah, but that was the objection, the stumblingblock, to Herbert—*single*. He would have been very well content to take old Thompson as his pattern, if his other companions had done so too: but to be linked in friendship with a young man who was perpetually being quizzed for his religion; to be pinned to his coat-sleeve, as their fellows would have said; perhaps to be called old Herbert—the idea was too monstrous. The sneering smile conquered him. He hastened to disclaim the dreadful notion that he was engaged to hear a sermon, or to go to any of old Thompson's whimsical resorts; and, after a faint resistance, he yielded his early prejudices, and disobeyed his father's affectionate injunctions. He went that night *only for once*, as he protested in secret to old Thompson. But no one should say, or think, "I will do what my conscience tells me I ought not to do, only once. I will not repel this temptation with all my strength; but I will exert all my powers against it next time." In spite of his misgivings, Herbert was fascinated with the amusement; no arguments or sneers were needed to prompt him to a second visit; and before long he became the inviter rather than the invited.

And what harm was there in it? Much, in many ways. By giving way to the allurements of the theatre, the weak-minded young man soon lost all relish for the business in which he was engaged. Day-books and ledgers were dull things, and to be writing all day long was tiresome work; and the consequence was, that Herbert became negligent of his duty, and made so many blunders in his books, as to call forth the frequent reprimands of his employer.

Then these frequent visits to the theatre broke in upon his proper hours of rest, and consumed a large part of the money that he received. Sleepless nights, after the dissipation of the evening, gave Herbert many a day's headache; and an exhausted purse gave him many an hour's heartache, which no remembrance of past pleasures, nor anticipation of future ones, could send away.

Conscience could not always be lulled to sleep in Herbert's breast. Although he tried to persuade himself that he was pursuing a very innocent amusement, he knew better than this. He could not but feel that very unholy passions were excited within him by what he heard and witnessed; that his remaining reverence for the Bible and the Sabbath was very fast diminishing; and that, in addition to this, he had made light of the injunctions of a father who loved him dearly, and sought only his advantage in the restrictions he had laid down. It was under the influence of depressing thoughts, such as these, that Herbert, more than once, said to himself, "I will never go to the theatre again." But then, if he were to refuse to go, he should be *laughed at!* This was too dreadful to be borne. To be called or thought a coward—it was not to be endured; so he acted the coward in reality!

But it was not in one particular alone that Herbert gave up his better judgment to the guidance and control of others, lest he should be thought a coward.

"Nonsense!" shouted a gay companion, in his ears, one Sunday morning; "you are not going to mope away your time in psalm-singing today? Leave that to old Thompson, my hearty, or go to church when the sun does not shine. See what a glorious day it is for a good stroll out of this smoky hole. Come, what do you say? Where shall we go?"

"I—I really cannot go with you today. I have a particular engagement;" stammered Herbert.

"Ah, I thought old Thompson had been at you; but you must give him the go-by for once."

"I cannot, indeed," replied Herbert in a rueful tone.

"But you must, I tell you;" —and so he did; for it was more terrible by half to be called "Old Thompson's shadow," than to break an engagement, and desecrate the Sabbath into the bargain. He was brave enough to do the latter, but he had not courage to bear the former. So the day—the first of a long series of mis-spent Sabbaths—was spent in pleasure-seeking. A steamboat conveyed the young men to Richmond; and the beautiful trees and green grass of Richmond hill—so like his own dear native village scenery, and so unlike the grim blackness of the city—reconciled poor Herbert to the violence done to his deadened conscience. Strange that the thoughts of home, stirred up by country scenes, should not have reminded him of Sabbath employments at home. Perhaps they did; but he soon got rid of the unwelcome guests.

Incited by one evil companion especially, and by others in a less degree, Herbert soon learned to mock at sin, and to laugh at his former scruples as unmanly and absurd. Having allowed himself to be tempted to *walk* in the counsel of the ungodly, and to *stand* in the way of sinners, he at length *sat* in the seat of the scornful. (Ps. i. 1.)

Three years of pleasure-seeking and Sabbath-breaking had hardened his heart against the reproaches of conscience, and made him indifferent to all beside, so that he stood well in the opinion of his false friends. And yet there were times when Herbert was not at ease with himself; when he would have given much to recall the past; when he had some faint wishes, at least, that he had given heed to the admonition, "If sinners entice thee, consent thou not." But the chains of habit were around him, and the allurements of evil were becoming stronger and stronger.

"Drink, drink, my boy, and drown your care!" Herbert had already drank enough to bewilder his brain; but not half enough to drown his care. He had that on his mind at this particular time which defied the power of wine and song. His irregularities had, that day, drawn upon him the severest rebukes of his employer; and the threat of dismissal was hanging over his head. He had received a letter from home, in which his father affectionately admonished him respecting some misbehaviour which had reached his ears; and urged him, by all the hopes which had once been formed of him, to forsake the paths of false pleasure, and return to the God of his mercies.

"I *will* return," was Herbert's first resolution, on reading that letter. "I will spend this evening alone, and in prayer."

The evening came, and found him in a tavern, with two of his dissolute companions. It would be cowardly—so reasoned the evil principle in his heart—to quail beneath the frowns of a precise old fellow like his employer, or to be melted into tenderness by a few soft words in a letter. Besides, if he were to show signs of such weakness, should he not be laughed at? He would bear any thing rather than that.

But Herbert had another cause for anxiety, which will presently appear.

"Drink, and drown your care," repeated one of his friends, seeing that he passed the bottle along without filling his glass.

"I believe I have had enough," replied poor Herbert.

"Not a bit of it; why, you look like a rated hound. What can be the matter with you?"

Herbert stammered out part of his trouble.

"Is that all?" said his tempter. "Then let us drink the old fellow's health in a bumper. Off with it, man. And suppose you do lose your situation; there are as good to be got, and better too, for asking. Look at me, now; why, when he slipped me off so unhandsomely, all I had to do was to step into the next street: better salary, more liberty, more life, and all that. Send you away! Much good may it do him. I half wish he would, for your sake. Come, another glass, my lad."

It was very true that Herbert's former fellow-clerk, having been dismissed from one counting-house for gross negligence, had speedily found another open for him. Herbert knew this before; and being now reminded of it, he began to think lightly of his own precarious standing with his employer. But Herbert did not know that his friend had already tired out his new employers; that he was on the brink of an exposure which must inevitably ruin his character; and that he was, at that very moment, seeking Herbert's cooperation in a scheme for his own escape, which, if it failed, would involve the hapless youth likewise in the same ruin.

"By the way, Herbert," he said; "suppose we change the subject. I owe you five pounds; do you want it just now?"

Indeed Herbert did want the five pounds; for, one of the causes of his gloom was, that his last quarter's salary had almost entirely disappeared, and that demands from more than one of his creditors had that very day been pressed upon him—demands which he had no means of satisfying. He had dreaded to remind his *friend* of this long-standing debt, lest he should be called mercenary. He was overjoyed, therefore, when the subject was introduced by that friend himself.

"If you can let me have it," replied Herbert, eagerly, "I shall be very glad of it; for, to tell the truth, I am very much in need; and I shall have nothing to receive for the next month."

"How very unfortunate!" was the rejoinder. "Now I have been hoping all along that you might have another five pounds to spare for a week or two, till my day comes round. And you really are worked out, eh?"

"Not ten shillings left," sighed Herbert.

"That purse of yours that you pulled out just now seemed too heavy for ten shillings," remarked the tempter, with a little degree of sharpness. "But perhaps you carry half-pence in your purse, to make believe with. A capital plan that," he continued, addressing their companion, who had hitherto been silent—"a good plan that, Ambrose."

But Herbert disclaimed such a practice. There was money in his purse, he said; but it was not his own. He had received it that afternoon from his employer, to pay a tradesman who lived near his lodgings. He ought to have called with it the same evening; but it would be too late now, and he must do it the first thing tomorrow.

His two companions winked significantly at each other; but said nothing. They presently called for more wine, and took care to ply the infatuated youth with fresh bumpers, until his cares and his reasons were alike for a time drowned. It was the first time Herbert had been really intoxicated; but not the first time, by many, that he had looked "upon the wine when it is red, when it giveth its color in the cup, when it moveth itself aright." (Prov. xxiii. 31.)

Of the rest of the proceedings of that evening, Herbert had but a very imperfect and confused recollection, when, at an hour past midnight, he was led by his *friends* to his lodgings, and laid his throbbing head on the pillow. In the morning, with returning consciousness, came that sinking of spirits which belongs pre-eminently to the drunkard, and that dread of consequences which no blustering can beat off from the conscience of the evil-doer. He first, instinctively almost, felt in his pocket for his purse. It was there, safe. He pulled it out, and counted its contents. Wonderful! So far from being diminished, it contained more by several pounds than on the preceding evening. Herbert sat down and pondered. He had an indistinct remembrance of reeling from the tavern, accompanied by his two boon companions; of passing along two or three well known streets, and then being led unresistingly up a dark passage which he had never before explored. Then he recollected something of a large room, brilliantly lighted, and crowded with guests, who seemed inclined to dispute his entrance until he was introduced in form by one of his friends. The rattling of dice, the sharp exclamations of the players, the muttered oaths of the losers, with many other kindred circumstances, convinced Herbert that he had spent some time in a gaming house; that he had lent money—not his own—to his friends; that he had staked it on his own account, and, strange to say, had won! These conjectures were confirmed beyond question, when, as he was proceeding to his employer's counting-house, he met one of his last night's companions, who congratulated him on their mutual good luck, and proposed an early repetition of the visit. Poor Herbert!

In a small village in the south of England is a neat cottage, inhabited by an aged couple, who are said to have seen better days, and by a middle aged man—their son. Deep lines of sorrow are marked on all their countenances; but on that of the son, there are also strong indications of premature old age.

"The old folks," say the villagers, "were well to do in the world once, far away from here; and their son was sent to the city to be a merchant. But he went on very badly, and was turned out of one or two situations; and at last was caught robbing his master—such a drunken, extravagant, gambling, dishonest fellow he became. So he was tried, and transported across the seas for fourteen years, though his poor father begged hard for him to be forgiven, and would have parted with all he had, so that his son might not be exposed and punished. Then things went badly with the old man: he lost heart, and came almost to ruin, only that he had an annuity, or something of that sort, coming in, that could not be touched. So they sold off every thing, and came to live here; and when their good-for-nothing son came home from transportation, they brought him down here, too. And oh, to see how kindly they treat him!"

This is the village story; and it is nearer the truth than many village stories are. That returned convict is Herbert—the boy who could not bear to be laughed at—who had not the courage to say NO.

Dear young readers, be warned by this example, and "let him that thinketh he standeth take heed lest he fall." Never fear to be singular—never dread the mockery of the foolish and sinful, because you will not go in their ways. It is better, far better, to be laughed to scorn by men, than to be frowned upon by God: and He has said, "Though hand join hand, the wicked shall not be unpunished;" that "He, that being often reproved hardeneth his neck, shall suddenly be destroyed, and that without remedy;" and that "As righteousness tendeth to LIFE: so he that pursueth evil pursueth it unto his own DEATH." (Prov. xxix. 1; xi. 19-21.)

THE END

THE LOST LAMB

D AISY DELAFIELD sat by the fire on a low stool with a book in her hand. It was a story-book, and upon the first page was printed in large letters, "The Lost Lamb," and then, in smaller type, "with illustrations." When this book was given to Daisy by her Aunt Fannie, she did not know the meaning of the word illustration; but she asked her aunt to explain it to her, and she was told that the illustrations were pictures put in the book to help the children who should read the story to understand it better.

Daisy was looking now at these illustrations, or pictures. She had heard the story so often that she knew it by heart, but she liked to think about it, and see the pictures. The first one showed a bright and happy-looking lamb, standing beside the shepherd; the next, a poor, frightened lamb hiding away for fear of being caught by a large, fierce lion; and the next, the same little terrified animal standing upon the very edge of a steep precipice. It had run away from the lion's den and was afraid to turn back upon the road over which it had come; and it could not go forward, for right in its way was the deep pit down which if it should fall it would certainly be dashed to pieces. Every time Daisy looked at this picture the tears came into her eyes, and she felt a choking in the throat. She knew perfectly well that the poor little lamb was neither eaten up by the great lion, nor crushed to death by falling into the pit; but still she found it hard to keep from crying at the very thought that one of these things might have happened to it.

At last, when she could hold her tears in no longer and was afraid of sobbing out loud, she turned over the leaves in a hurry to the last picture, which was very beautiful and comforting. Here she saw the lost lamb safe and sound in the arms of the good shepherd, who had been out looking for the little wanderer, and had found it just at the right moment to save it from danger.

This story of "The Lost Lamb" was a favorite one with Daisy, and her mother often talked to her about it, showing her the lesson which it was meant to teach. She was told that Jesus is the Good Shepherd, and that little children are the lambs of his flock—weak and helpless, and very likely to get lost, just like real lambs; that Satan the wicked one—goes about like a roaring lion, trying to catch them by persuading them to sin, which will lead them into even worse harm than they could find in a lion's den; that there are temptations to do wrong all around them, which are quite as dangerous as the deepest pit into which they could fall; and the only one who can save from these is the Good Shepherd.

They wander away from him and get lost, but he keeps looking for them and calling them, and they must listen for his voice and trust themselves to his care, and then they will be sure to be safe, no matter what happens. Then Daisy said to her mother:

"Jesus does not speak to me as he did to those who went about with him when he lived in this world, and then how can I hear him even if I do listen?"

"When I tell you to listen to him, my dear," her mother answered, "I mean that you must attend to all that he says to you in the Bible. He does not live on the earth and go about talking to the people as he once did; but he talks to us through the Bible, which is full of his words. From it we learn what he would like to have us do, and therefore we ought to read and study it, and listen when others read it, so that we may know how to please him. We must listen, too, when those who know more about him than we do tell us about him, and we must pray to him to teach us, and we must trust ourselves to his care. We may wander far away from him by doing wrong, and then, as soon as we see this, instead of going still farther away by doing worse, we must come back to him by feeling sorry for our sins, and giving them up immediately."

Her mother went on to tell her much more about Jesus, the Good Shepherd—how very kind he is to the lambs of his flock; how very dearly he loves them, and how he even died to save them. The good shepherd in the story-book loved the little

111

lamb, even after it was so naughty as to leave the green pastures, where he kept it safe from harm, to go away and wander off by itself into the road and woods, where there were so many dangers. He mourned for it, fearing that it might fall in the pit or be eaten up by the roaring lion, and he went out to look for it, never resting until he found it and brought it back again to the beautiful green fields where the flock dwelt. But this shepherd did not put himself in to the lion's way, to be torn to pieces to save its life; this our Good Shepherd has done for us. Ah, how very much we ought to love him!

Daisy listened attentively to all that her mother said, and very often when she looked at the pretty pictures in her story-book, she thought of Jesus, her own Good Shepherd, and of all that he had done for her.

DAISY'S right name was Theodosia, and she was named after her grandmother; but as Theodosia was so long and hard to say, she was nearly always called Daisy. She had no sisters, and only one brother, a very large boy, several years older than herself, who was named Thomas, but generally called Tom. Daisy was very fond of walking out in the streets with Thomas, but it was not often that she could do so. He said that he liked very much to have her company, but that it was inconvenient. He went to school every morning, and he had a number of engagements for the afternoons. In summer it was fishing, or swimming, or base-ball, and in the winter it was skating.

Daisy used sometimes to think that if he liked her company so much as he pretended, he might take her with him to the ball-ground or skating, as she had often promised him that if he would do so, she would stand or sit in the spot where he would put her, and never move from it, or do anything but look on until he should be ready to go home. But Tom said that it would not do; that a little girl had no business at such places, and would be in the way; and that he could not be bothered.

One bright September morning, however, he came to the nursery door and looking in, said:

"Come, little sister, get your traps on, for I am going to Market Street on an errand for mother, and I am to take you with me."

Daisy knew that when Tom said "traps" he meant her hat and jacket, so she ran off as fast as she could to get them. When she was quite dressed and ready to go, her mother went to the door with her, and kissing her good-bye, said:

"Now, Daisy my dear, keep very near to your brother, and do not lose sight of him, or you may get lost."

"Yes, ma'am," Daisy answered, taking Tom's hand.

In this way, hand in hand, they left the house together, but they had not gone far when they met a very large boy, named Ralph Miller, who went to school with Tom.

"Hallo! Tom Delafield!" he called out, as soon as he saw him, "Where did you come from? Been out hunting Indians, hey? and captured a papoose? Well, that's right; hold on to it tightly, or it may get loose and escape to its native forests."

Daisy did not remember ever before to have heard the word *papoose*, but she guessed rightly that it meant a small Indian, and she was not very well pleased that the name should be given to her. Her hair and eyes were very black, and her skin was darker than Tom's; for Tom looked like their mother, while she was like their father. Tom called her Marigold, and her father, "his little brown Daisy" sometimes on this account; and a lady visitor had called her a brunette; but she was not an Indian, and Ralph had no right to say that she was one. She felt afraid of him and clung still closer to her brother, who had tried to loosen her grasp of his hand.

Having finished his rude speech, Ralph seemed to have no more to say, and went on his way, leaving Daisy surprised and uncomfortable, and her brother not quite easy.

"How very tight you are holding on to my hand!" he said presently; "you seem to be bearing the whole of your weight on me."

Now the whole of Daisy's weight was not so very heavy but that Tom could have easily borne it; and he was in the habit of lifting her up and boasting of how far he could carry her. It was not her weight that troubled him, but he was foolish enough to be disturbed by Ralph's coarse speech. He was afraid of meeting more of his boy friends, and hearing other remarks of the same kind. Daisy did not let go of his hand altogether, but she held it very lightly. Tom was still not satisfied, and in a few moments he spoke again very sharply:

"I do wish you would let go of my hand, Daisy; you are not a baby; you can walk alone if you try."

Tears came into Daisy's eyes. Ralph's rudeness had frightened and astonished her, but she could not have cried over it, for he was a rough, coarse boy, and she did not like him. But it was very different with Thomas, who was her brother, and whom she dearly loved. She could not bear to have him speak crossly to her, so she instantly dropped his hand and walked on silently. After a while, Tom began to feel ashamed of himself. He did not tell Daisy this, but commenced talking pleasantly to her about the things they passed, and telling her little stories; and Daisy saw that he was not angry with her, and brightened up considerably.

They went on a block or two farther until they reached a part of Chestnut Street where there were a number of high stores, whose windows were filled with pretty things. Here Thomas met two of his friends, whom he had not seen for a long time, and the three boys stood on one side of the pavement to have a good talk together. Daisy went over to a store window; but there was nothing in it except men's coats and vests, and she did not care to look at these.

"I will go a little farther to another store," she said, "and I will still be near enough to see Tom."

So on she went until she came to the next window, but it belonged to a "gentleman's furnishing store," and there was nothing very pretty in it either. She looked back at Tom, still busy with his friends, and walked farther. Her next stopping-place was at a bookseller's window, and here she was delighted with the books and pictures. She spelled over the names on the backs of the books, and looked at the pictures for what seemed to her a very long time. There was an advertisement hanging in one of the large panes of glass, with "A boy wanted" printed in large letters. She read this and wondered at first what the bookseller wanted with a boy, but concluded it must be to run errands and sell books. What a nice place it must be for a boy! she thought. He could read pretty books and see pictures all day, except just when he was sent on errands, and that would be taking pleasant walks, as she was doing then. She wished she was a boy.

While she was thinking of this she heard a stir very near to her, and upon turning saw a man, with an organ on his back, carrying a monkey. Of all animals in the world, there was none more attractive to Daisy than a monkey. She was not particularly fond of monkeys, for she was too little acquainted with them for this; but she was very curious about them, and they interested her very much. This one had such an old, withered face, and wore a funny little hat with a red feather, and blue clothes with gilt buttons, which made him look so queer that she wanted very much to see him walking. A crowd of boys and girls followed the man; and although Daisy was timid in a crowd, yet she now joined in with them, hurrying along, her eyes fixed on the monkey, and her mind too full of it to allow even fear to disturb her. The man walked on very fast, never once stopping, as the children hoped he would do. He was hungry, and on his way home to his dinner, but they did not know this, and still followed, running to keep up with him.

Daisy after the Organ Man

DAISY began to grow very tired of running, and found it hard to keep up with the crowd. The monkey, with its owner, had got far ahead of her, but she kept her eye on the red feather until it disappeared round the corner of a street, and then her strength and courage left her, and she gave up in despair. All hopes of seeing the monkey at his capers being gone, for the first time she remembered her brother.

"I wonder where Tom can be?" she said to herself, looking all around her.

But Tom was nowhere to be seen, and she walked hurriedly on, not knowing what way she was taking. On and on she went; her poor little feet were aching, but she did not much care for this, if only she might find her brother Tom.

"Oh dear!" she said, when she could still see nothing of him "—oh, dear! I am lost, and what shall I do? I am afraid that I shall never see my mother and father again; and I have been naughty and disobeyed my mother, for she told me to be sure not to leave Tom. A roaring lion may come and eat me up, or I may fall into a pit."

You need not laugh at Daisy for thinking of a lion catching her, since lions are not seen running through the city streets. She knew this as well as you do; but there was a zoo of wild animals on exhibition in town, and she had once heard a story of a wild animal breaking loose from its cage; and, knowing that she had been a disobedient little girl and deserved punishment, she was afraid that the lion might escape from its keepers to punish her. A guilty conscience is very likely to make people easily frightened. She felt as if she would be glad to hide herself, if she only knew where; but she did not, and so went wandering along.

Confused and troubled and uncertain which way to take, she turned into another street; and here almost the first thing that she saw was a policeman. Now next to a lion, Daisy was afraid of a policeman; and this man was very tall, and looked to her even taller than he was.

"Oh dear!" she cried out once more, looking around to find some way of escape, "what shall I do?"

The next moment she spied out a narrow court, and she ran into this to hide, trembling from head to foot. But the policeman had not noticed her at all, and peeping out, she saw his tall figure passing down the street. In a little while, she mustered courage to come out from her hiding-place, again to look around and consider what she should do. Among all the people who hurried past her, there was not one whom she had ever seen before—not one to whom she could tell her troubles, and she was all alone. She remembered the poor little lost lamb, and how frightened it was before the shepherd found it. Would anyone find her before something dreadful should happen to her, she wondered. The tears streamed down her cheeks, and she thought of what her mother had told her about the Good Shepherd, who had died to save her. He would know what she said if she cried to him only in her heart, and if he was willing to die for her, he would certainly hear and help her if she asked him. She might not be able to see him, for he was a spirit, and we cannot see a spirit, but she was sure he could hear her prayer.

She shut her eyes and whispered, "Oh, dear Jesus! Be my Good Shepherd, and take care of me and help me to find my brother."

Then she opened her eyes, and although they were still full of tears, yet she was not so much afraid as she had been.

CHAPTER IV

DAISY walked only a few steps forward after she had prayed when someone touched her on the shoulder. She felt a little frightened just then, and looked up hastily; but she saw only a gentleman, with a very kind and pleasant face.

"What is the matter, my dear little girl?" he asked, in a very gentle voice.

Daisy looked up at him, and felt in a moment that she could trust him, and all her fears were gone.

"I lost my brother," she said, "and I cannot find my way home."

Here Daisy began to cry more than ever, but the tears made her feel better.

"Never mind, my dear," said the gentleman, taking her hand and soothing her; "come with me, and if we do not find your brother, I dare say we shall be able to find your home."

They were standing before a very nice confectionery store, with some handsome cakes and fruit in the window. The gentleman looked in at these for a moment and then turning to Daisy, said, "I suppose you like cakes and peaches, and ice cream?"

"Oh yes, sir, very much indeed," Daisy answered.

Only a few minutes before, when Daisy passed that same window, she never once thought of the nice things that were in it; and her heart was so full of fear and trouble that she could not have eaten the finest cakes or the best ice cream in the world. Now, however, she felt much easier, and sure that all would soon be right.

"Very well," said the gentleman, "as you like good things, and I do too, we might as well go into this store and get some. We will take them near the open door, where we can see your brother if he should pass; and while we are eating you can tell me your name and where you live."

Daisy went in with the gentleman, and he asked for some peaches, cakes and ice cream, and they sat down at a table near to the door to eat them.

"Now you must tell me your name," said the gentleman.

"Daisy Delafield," replied Daisy. But she did not speak very distinctly, and the gentleman thought the last name sounded like Duffield; so he repeated after her, "Daisy Duffield?"

"No, sir," said Daisy; "it is Daisy Delafield."

"Oh yes, I know now," said he—"Daisy Dayfield."

Daisy heard the mistake that he made, but she did not correct it. Dayfield was very nearly like Delafield, and she did not know that she could make the name sound any clearer to him.

"You have a Directory, I suppose?" said the gentleman to a boy who just then brought up a waiter with two tumblers of water.

"Yes, sir, we have," replied the boy. He went away to get it, leaving Daisy full of wonder as to what a Directory could be. It might be something good to eat that she had never tasted, and she was full of curiosity to see it. Presently the boy came back, but he only brought with him a very large book, which he laid upon the table. The gentleman took it up, and turning over the leaves, said,

"Now, Daisy, perhaps you can tell me your father's first name?"

"Yes, sir," Daisy answered; "it is Lewis."

"Does he keep a store?" inquired the gentleman.

"Yes sir," said Daisy, "and he sells money, I think."

The gentleman opened his eyes very wide, and looked quite curious.

"Sells money?" he repeated.

"Yes, sir," replied Daisy, very seriously, "for I have been to his store with Tom; and people came in, and he gave them money, and he had nothing there but a high desk and chairs, and a green table, and drawers with papers and money."

"Nothing else?" asked the gentleman.

"Oh yes, books; I forgot them," said Daisy.

"Perhaps he is in a bank," said the gentleman, as if he were speaking to himself; and then in a louder tone he said to Daisy, "Was it a very large room, and were there other gentlemen there with high desks?"

"Oh no," said Daisy, looking around; "the room was not as big as this, and there was no one but himself and Mr. Smith. I like Mr. Smith very much. Do you know him?"

"Very likely," replied the gentleman, still looking at the book; "but I had rather his name was not Smith."

Daisy thought this was queer. Smith was a good name to her, and she did not know that the gentleman wanted very much to find out her home, and that he only wished that there were not so many Mr. Smiths, thinking that it might help him to do so. The big book, or Directory, contained the names of almost all the grown-up people in the city, the business they followed, and where they lived. He had been examining it, and could find but one "Dayfield"—John Dayfield, "milkman;" and he felt pretty sure that this could not be Daisy's father. Daisy did not know why he was anxious, but she saw his worried look, and she thought she would try to amuse him by talking to him, and making herself as agreeable as possible.

"Are you a shepherd?" she asked, by way of commencement.

He looked up at her in astonishment at the question, and said, "Well, no; I cannot say that I am; although I do happen to deal in wool."

"Then how did you come to find me?" Daisy again asked.

The gentleman still did not seem to understand her; so she went on to tell him about her storybook of the "Lost Lamb" and all it suffered and how the good shepherd found it at last and took it safely home.

"That is a very pretty story," said the gentleman.

"Do you know what it means?" inquired Daisy.

"I am not quite sure," replied the gentleman, "but I think you do, and I would like you to tell me."

Then Daisy told him what her mother had taught her about Jesus being her Good Shepherd, and of Satan—the wicked one-going about like a roaring lion, trying to lead the stray lambs into harm by persuading them to do wrong.

The gentleman looked very grave, and Daisy hastened to comfort him by saying, "But you need not be afraid of *him*."

"Who? the bad man?" asked the gentleman.

"I did not call him the bad man," said Daisy, correcting him. "I called him the wicked *one*. Satan is a spirit, not a man, or else we might see him sometimes and get out of his way; but he is a spirit, and very deceitful. Yet you need not be afraid of him, for Jesus is ever so much stronger than he is, and can save you from him, if you will pray for it. Mother says as soon as ever anyone finds that they are doing wrong, that instead of going on in the same way, and doing worse, that they must just tell Jesus right away that they are very sorry, and ask him to please to take care of them, and then Satan cannot even touch them to hurt them."

Daisy looked into the gentleman's face once more, but it was just as grave as ever, and she was afraid that he did not believe what she said, because she was such a little girl.

"It is all true," she continued. "Jesus really will take care of you. He loved us so well that he was willing to die on the dreadful cross to save us. It is all written down in the Bible and you can see it there for yourself. Do you read the Bible every day?"

"Not every day," replied the gentleman.

"What a pity!" said Daisy; "then perhaps you did not know how kind Jesus is to us; and it is a good thing that you found me, for I can tell you all about it, for my mother has taught it to me. But I think you had better read it for yourself in the Bible."

"Yes, I think I had," the gentleman answered; "but what made you ask me if I was a shepherd?"

"Well," replied Daisy, "when I could not see Tom anywhere, and found that I was really lost, I felt very much frightened. I remembered the story of the 'Lost Lamb,' and what mother had told me of Jesus, the Good Shepherd, and that when I was afraid, and did not know what I should do, I might pray to him to help me, for he would be sure to hear me. So I shut my eyes and asked him to take care of me, and very soon you came along and found me. I knew that Jesus had sent you, and I thought that maybe you were a shepherd. Not the Good Shepherd, but the sort of shepherd my story-book tells about—the one that found the poor little stray lamb when it was on the very edge of the deep pit."

"You are right in one thing, at any rate," said the gentleman.

"What was that?" Daisy asked.

"In thinking that Jesus sent me to you," he replied.

"Why, yes," said Daisy, "I knew that all the time."

CHAPTER V

DAISY was feeling quite comfortable just now. She was very much at home with the gentleman, and she was pleased to think she had been able to do him a good turn by telling him all about the Good Shepherd. The ice cream and cakes, too, were very nice, and now she was about to try the peaches.

She had only taken her first bite out of one of them when she looked over toward the door, and to her great astonishment there stood Tom, anxiously beckoning to her. I am almost ashamed to tell you that Daisy was sorry, instead of being glad, to see her brother. She turned her head away uneasily, determined to appear not to notice him; but it would not do, and she found herself every now and then throwing sly glances toward the door, where Tom still stood, doing his best to get her to come out to him.

It may seem strange to you that Thomas Delafield, who was almost a man, and stood at the top of nearly every class in his school, should be very shy of strangers. But this was really the case and this was the reason why he now stood beckoning at the store door, instead of coming boldly in and telling the gentleman that Daisy was his sister.

And what shall I say of Daisy's conduct in pretending not to see him? There is only one thing that can be said, and that perhaps would not be called an excuse. It is this: Daisy Delafield was very fond of cakes and peaches, and there were still some of both left on the plates, and she wished in her heart that Tom had only stayed away until she had eaten them all.

But the gentleman at length noticed the queer faces she was making, and looking toward the door to find out what caused them, he saw Tom.

"Do you know that boy, Daisy?" he asked.

Daisy could not tell a lie, of course, so she was obliged to tell the truth.

"Yes, sir; it is our Tom," she said, speaking in a very low tone.

"Oh! is it?" said the gentleman, instantly going over to the door to bring Tom in. He came presently back to where Daisy sat, bringing Tom with him.

"Come, Daisy," said her brother; "I am very glad to have found you, but we must hurry home or mother will be frightened."

Daisy looked longingly at the cakes and peaches.

"Oh, I wish you had not found me for ever so long, Tom," she said.

The gentleman smiled, and left them to say something to a young girl who stood behind the counter. She took down from a nail a neat-looking little basket, and filling it with cakes and fruit and some sugar-plums, handed it to him.

He came back with it to Daisy and said, "Here, my dear little Daisy, is a basket for you; you may keep the basket when you have finished eating what is in it, and perhaps it may help to remind you of the pleasant hour we have spent here this morning."

Then turning to Thomas, he invited him to sit down and have some ice cream and cakes, but Thomas would not wait to eat anything.

"I tried to find your name in the Directory," the gentleman continued, "but there was only one 'Dayfield,' and I concluded that he could not be the person."

"Our name is not Dayfield, but Delafield," replied Thomas; "my father is a broker, and I know his name is in the Directory, for I have seen it there."

The strange gentleman was so very gentle in his manners that even Thomas forgot his shyness, and spoke out boldly.

"Delafield!" the gentleman exclaimed; "is it possible? Why, I am well acquainted with your father in a business way, and have often been at his office. I thought this little girl told me that her name was 'Dayfield.'"

"No sir" Daisy answered. "I said—"

Here she tried to say the name very distinctly, but it did not sound any more like Delafield than it had done the first time.

"I see," the gentleman said very politely; "I did not understand you, and it was my mistake; but for fear of any further mistakes between us, I will give you my name in writing."

Here he took a card from his pocket and handed it to Thomas, saying,

"Show this to your father, and tell him that his little daughter has afforded me a very pleasant and profitable hour that I shall not soon forget. She has given me very good advice."

Daisy was pleased to hear the gentleman say these things of her. He had used different words from what she would have done, but she understood their meaning on the whole very well. I do not think that any face could have looked much happier than did Daisy Delafield's when she bade the gentleman good-bye, and thanked him over and over again for the basket of fruit, which she carried so carefully.

"Good-bye," said the gentleman, "and I hope that we shall meet again very soon."

After a while, when Daisy and her brother were on their way home, Thomas took out the card and read the name— "Henry Lawrence, Jr." He had heard of Mr. Henry Lawrence, Jr., before, he told Daisy.

Mrs. Delafield was very glad to see her son and daughter once more, for she had grown quite anxious about them. When Daisy was telling her story, she felt very uncomfortable in being obliged to say that the way in which she got lost was through disobeying her mother, and running after a monkey, instead of keeping near to her brother. When she spoke of her distress and fear at finding herself all alone in the street, and *lost*, just like the poor little lamb she had read of, the tears started to her eyes.

"And mother," she said, keeping back the sobs, "I remembered what you told me and prayed to Jesus, the Good Shepherd, and he sent Mr. Henry Lawrence to take care of me and give me all these nice things."

"I am delighted to hear it," said her mother.

Then Daisy went on to tell all about the handsome confectionery store, and Mr. Lawrence and the Directory. She seemed to have seen and noticed everything; even to a row of tin jelly-moulds ranged upon a high shelf, and one of which was the shape of a very queer bird, that appeared to have no legs. Daisy had never seen anything like it in life.

"My dear child," said Mrs. Delafield, when she had finished, "you must ask God to help you to be more obedient to your mother in the future. He was very good to you this time in sending you such a kind friend; but we must not sin that good may come, or he will be very angry. If you should get lost again through disobedience as you were today, it will show that you were not truly sorry for having done wrong. Your hymn says,

> 'Repentance is to leave
> The sins we loved before,
> And show that we in earnest grieve,
> By doing so no more.'

"It is not every little lost girl who falls into such good hands, and another time you might not fare so well."

"I do not wish to do wrong, mother," said Daisy, "and get lost again, even if I should get cakes and ice cream and peaches. It is a dreadful thing to be lost, and I think I can pity the poor little lost lamb more now than ever I did."

THE GOOD SHEPHERD

"WHEN I was a girl about your age," said mamma to her little Mary, "I lived up among the hills with my grandfather, and I will tell you what happened one winter to a shepherd who stayed at the foot of the hill, during a snowstorm. It will make you understand what a good shepherd must do.

"My grandfather's house stood about half a mile from the shepherd's cottage. It was an old house, with great thick walls and small windows; a few old trees stood round and sheltered it from the storm. But it was very comfortable inside; I remember the dining-room, with a large, wide fireplace, and all the walls paneled with oak boards and polished bright with varnish; how cheery it looked when the blazing fire roared up the chimney, and grandfather took me on his knee after dinner to tell me a story! There was no other house near the shepherd's cottage for many miles; all was high hills and green valleys, where the sheep fed.

"One evening, soon after Christmas-time, the snow began to fall in little white flakes; then it went off again; but great clouds were gathered up in the north, and soon quietly, but heavily, the snow began again. Next morning it had covered everything with a thick white mantle. It snowed all that day and part of the next day, and then a cold wind began to blow; and the snow was so deep and so dry that the wind drifted up all the windows and doors of our house, and almost hid the cottage altogether. We could not get out at our back door at all.

"I was tired with being shut up; and I was standing at the window after tea, breathing on the glass, and clearing a little spot to look out at, when I saw a little black speck moving near the cottage slowly through the snow. 'What is that moving at the cottage?' I asked grandfather.

"'It is James himself going out to look after his sheep. This wind would soon drift the snow over the sheep and smother them, for the sheep always go to the sheltered side of the hill, and there the snow gathers thickest; therefore, though it is so cold and so deep with snow, the shepherd must go and take his sheep to a safe place. The worse the storm is, the more danger to the sheep, and the more the need of the shepherd.'

"'This is a fearful night; I hope James will take care of himself,' was the reply. But James never returned to his cottage! The next morning his wife anxiously looked for his return, the storm set in again, and toward evening she made her way to our house to tell us her sad fears. All who could go out set out, but the snow had hid his footsteps, and they soon returned in wait for morning. All search was fruitless till the snow melted, when his body was found at the foot of a crag, his faithful dog watching near, though hardly able to crawl. At a little distance a dead lamb was found, and it was supposed he had been attempting to carry the lamb to a place of safety, when, through darkness and drifting snow, he had missed the path and fallen over the rock. James was a good shepherd.

"Now, I will tell you how you and I are like these poor sheep, and how Christ is like a good shepherd.

"We are like these sheep, first, because we are sinners, and God's just wrath, like the dreadful storm, is ready to destroy us. Second, because we try to forget this, and this just makes our ruin more sure. So the sheep stupidly go where their destruction is certain.

"Christ is like a good shepherd, first, because he seeks to save us from the punishment due to us for our sins, and make us good and happy. Second, because he gave his life to do this; he died on the cross for us.

"Will you not love that Good Shepherd, and do what he bids you? Then you may say with David, 'The Lord is my shepherd: I shall not want.'"

See, Israel's gentle Shepherd stands
With all-engaging charms;
Hark, how he calls the tender lambs,
And folds them in his arms.

"Permit them to approach," he cries,
Nor scorns their humble name:
For 'twas to bless such souls as these
The Lord of angels came.

He'll lead us to the heavenly streams,
Where living waters flow;
And guide us to the fruitful fields,
Where trees of knowledge grow.

The feeblest lamb amidst the flock
Shall be its Shepherd's care;
While folded in the Saviour's arms,
We're safe from every snare.

1. *Who is the Good Shepherd?* – The Lord Jesus Christ. He claims the title for himself.

2. *Who are the lost sheep?* – Sinners. They are called lost sheep, because they, like lost sheep, have wandered from Him who alone can protect them: they are defenseless and sure to be destroyed, unless they are saved by the Good Shepherd.

3. *What does the Good Shepherd do for his sheep?* – Seeks them, brings them back, feeds, guards, and dies for them. All this Jesus does for sinners.

4. *Who are Christ's sheep?* – Those who follow him and find him for their shepherd.

5. *How may you become one of Christ's sheep?* – By listening to his call, and crying to him to save you. He will do it, for he loves the lambs of his flock.

6. *Where shall Christ's flock be gathered together at last?* – In heaven. All Christ's sheep will be gathered there—no wolf, no thief can enter,—he will lead them by green pastures and living waters.

BIBLE VERSES

Sunday. Know ye that the Lord he is God: it is he that hath made us, and not we ourselves; we are his people, and the sheep of his pasture. – Ps. c. 3.

Monday. I have gone astray like a lost sheep. Seek thy servant, for I do not forget thy commandments. – Ps. cxix. 176.

Tuesday. If a man have an hundred sheep, and one of them be gone astray, doth he not leave the ninety-and-nine, and seeketh that which is gone astray? – Matt. xviii. 12.

Wednesday. The Lord is my shepherd; I shall not want. – Ps. xxiii. 1.

Thursday. My sheep hear my voice, and I know them, and they follow me. – John x. 27.

Friday. I am the good shepherd; the good shepherd giveth his life for the sheep. – John x. 11.

Saturday. And he shall set the sheep on his right hand. – Matt. xxv. 33.

MORNING AND EVENING VERSES

MORNING VERSES

I.

'Thou art my God; early will I seek thee.
Psalm lxiii. 1.

ANOTHER night of sweet repose;
Again I wake in peace;
O God, I bless thy holy name,
Whose mercies never cease.

Each day thou dost with tender love
Rich blessings on me pour;
I love thee, Lord; but oh I would
That I could love thee more!

Let all my words and all my ways
Declare that I am thine;
That so the light of truth and grace
Before the world may shine.

Oh never let me, Lord, forget
That Christ has died for me;
And may this thought constrain my soul
To live and die to thee.

II.

I will sing aloud of thy mercy in the morning.
Psalm lix. 16.

I THANK thee, Lord, for quiet rest,
And for thy care of me;
Oh let me through this day be blest,
And kept from harm by thee.

Oh take an evil heart away,
And make me pure and good;
Lord Jesus, save my soul, I pray,
And cleanse me by thy blood.

Help me to please my parents dear,
And do whate'er they tell:
Bless all my friends, both far and near,
And keep them safe and well.

III.

"O Lord, in the morning will I direct my prayer
unto thee."
Psalm v. 3.

KEEP me, gracious God, this day:
Dangers press around my way.
Let no sin an entrance find
To pollute my youthful mind.
Guard my soul from every snare,
Keep me with thy loving care.

Whither shall a sinner fly
When temptation hovers nigh?
Unto Jesus Christ alone:
He the tempter's power has known.
Feeling weakness, I would rest
On my Saviour's tender breast.
May his wisdom, grace and truth
Guide me through the snares of youth.

EVENING VERSES

IV.

"Evening and morning, and at noon, will I pray."
Psalm lv. 17.

—

FOR the mercies of this day
Thanks to thee, my God, I pay;
Now, ere I retire to rest,
Let my soul by thee be blest.

Through each dark and silent hour
Oh preserve me by thy power;
Keep me safe from every fear,
Thankful that my God is near.

Let the sins which I have done
All be pardon'd through thy Son,
From whose dying sacrifice
All my hopes and joys arise.

V

*"I will both lay me down in peace, and sleep: for
thou, Lord, only makest me dwell in safety."*
Psalm iv. 8.

—

BLESSED Saviour, hear me now;
Lowly at thy feet I bow.
Let thy watchful care this night
Keep me safe till morning light.

Lord, bestow a grateful heart
For the gifts thou dost impart
To a little child like me,
Who depends alone on thee.

All my sins, O Lord, forgive;
Fit me with thyself to live
In that glorious home above,
Purchased by thy dying love.

SABBATH MORNING

VI

"This is the day the Lord hath made."
Psalm cxviii. 24.

AWAKE, awake, your bed forsake,
To God your praises pay:
The morning sun is clear and bright,
With joy we hail his cheerful light:
In songs of love,
Praise God above,
It is the Sabbath-day.

VII

"Call the Sabbath a delight." – Isaiah lviii. 13.

Lord of the Sabbath, I rejoice
Thy holy day to see;
May I, assisted by thy grace,
Begin this week with thee.

I go this day to hear thy word
To sing, to pray and praise;
To learn of thee, my gracious Lord,
Religion's pleasant ways.

Oh may the Holy Spirit bless
These sacred means of grace;
That I might learn thy righteousness,
And seek in youth thy face.

Let all below and all above
Worship before thy face,
For ever praise the Saviour's love
And bless the Father's grace.

SABBATH EVENING

VIII

"A day in thy courts is better than a thousand."
Psalm lxxxiv. 10.

I'VE past another Sabbath-day,
And heard of Jesus and of heaven;
I thank thee for thy word, and pray
That Sabbath sins may be forgiven.

May all I heard and understood
Be well remember'd through the week,
And help to make me wise and good,
More humble, diligent and meek.

So, when my life is finish'd here,
And days and Sabbaths shall be o'er,
May I at thy right hand appear,
To serve and love thee evermore.

THE END

THE DEATH OF EMILY

IT matters little to the stranger to know who the subject of the following story was, or where she dwelt. It is enough to know that she was a simple Scottish girl whom the Saviour sought and saved. In this story of her early grace there is no colouring. The half has not been told.

Emily was not one who from infancy knew the Lord. The first years of childhood were passed away, and she had spent nearly fourteen years of her short life, before her feet began to tread the narrow way. Disease had begun to weaken her frame, before any relish for the things of Christ appeared. Previous to her last lingering illness of six months, there is little of interest to record. What follows relates to this period alone.

It was in the middle of August, 1846, that I was first privileged to visit this dear child. Mr. Bonar had gone to see her as soon as he heard of her illness, but, from what he knew of her before, his surprise and joy were great, to find her rejoicing in a new-found Saviour, and a Father reconciled. He left home for some weeks at this period, and it was in his absence that I began to visit her. She expressed herself with much simplicity with regard to her own unworthiness, and the completeness of the

righteousness which she had found in her
Redeemer. Her song at this time was literally,—

"I've found the pearl of greatest price,
And I must sing for joy."

I thought I never had seen a more beautiful
illustration of what faith really is,—a childlike
taking of God at his word, and casting all on him,
because he has desired it. She was much pleased
with the story of the poor idiot, whose only ray of
intelligence gleamed out in the rhyme he constantly
repeated,—

"I am a poor sinner and nothing at all,
But Jesus Christ is my all in all."

She often applied this poem to herself in the
times of her greatest weakness. She spoke with great
gratitude of her former Sabbath-school teacher, then
absent. She said her exhortations, though apparently
unfruitful at the time, had often impressed her
solemnly, and that during a short illness previously,
they had been brought back to her remembrance,
and she believed, blessed as the means of leading
her to Jesus. One day, some time after, when
speaking to me of a little Bible class which I had
commended to her prayers, she said, "Never give up
hoping, though you do not see one girl that seems
taking your words to heart. Think of me, and that
will mind you that maybe the Holy Spirit is working

where you cannot see. Or he may bring these truths to their remembrance, many days after you've thought them all forgot."

I asked her if she had not valued instruction at the time she received it in the class. "Oh!" she said, "I often used to tremble at what I heard, yet I turned careless again, and laughed it off with my companions. But God would not let me die; he laid his hand on me before it was too late, and surely I should love him, for am I not a brand plucked from the burning?"

The absence of her dear teacher and of her minister was a trial to her, at this early stage of what was thought to be a rapid decline. The former she saw no more in the body, though through her sister, affectionate messages frequently passed between them. She was spared to see the return of the latter, and to enjoy many of his visits.

Her life was prolonged beyond all expectation, I believe, to perfect the work of faith and love in her faithful, loving, but new-born spirit. She rallied in the end of autumn, and for a time, her friends were almost deceived into the idea that she was to continue among them. She could then sit up for hours together, reading, or doing a little work, as she was able. Yet never could those who watched her spiritual state with far greater anxiety than that of her body, discern anything like exultation, or a return to the friendship of the world, with this partial return to health. Pilgrim's Progress was her favorite companion, next to her Bible, and the Bible

Hymn Book, which was hardly ever out of her hand, or off her pillow, in her last illness. She had some new hymn to repeat to me at every visit, and it was interesting to observe her selection of those which breathed but of redeeming love, and the hope of the redeemed in death. She used to say, "I'm *feared* to be tried with the world again. I would rather be laid down again on that sick-bed, which Jesus made so pleasant to me, than get strong, and live to dishonour him."

He took her at her word. This delicate and only half-revived blossom seemed to droop under the first blighting frost. She was again confined to bed, with a return of every threatening symptom of her disease. Patiently she bore the change, calmly she spoke of the early death which awaited her, and joyfully anticipated the glory that should follow. I felt it a great privilege to visit her almost daily, for the last few weeks of her life, sometimes to bear to her a message of refreshment and consolation, but oftener, to receive refreshment from her dying lips, and to have my heart cheered by witnessing her visible progress from grace to grace, and from strength to strength.

It was delightful to see her daily growth in grace, and in the likeness of Christ. It seemed as if her eye was ever fixed on him, his name for ever on her lips, till much of his image and of his Spirit was reflected on her heart. Her constant words were, even after a night of sore coughing and pain, "still hoping in Jesus," "still happy in Jesus!" She said the nights did not seem long to her, while communing with her God, or repeating some of the many chapters, and psalms or hymns with which her mind was happily stored.

Her affection was strong, and her disappointment great, if she missed her usual visit. Never shall I forget the bright welcome which shone from her dark eye, each time I approached her bed, and the warmth with which she grasped my hand and retained it, generally till I rose to take leave, latterly clasped in both of hers, as if afraid to lose it.

The smile which invariably lighted her pale features, during her last illness, at first was *peaceful*, but for the last two weeks of her life, it was far more, it was full of unutterable joy. It was touching to mark the gradual decline of one so young, under the pressure of her wasting malady; yet the deeper she got in the swellings of Jordan, she was but the more exalted in spirit over all doubts and fears. The apostle's words were most true of her—that while the outward man perished, yet the inward man was renewed day by day! (2 Cor. iv. 16.) She seemed to be lying at the outside of the heavenly city, full in view of its golden gates, and already to catch some notes of the song of the redeemed.

I never saw such a complete absence of fear of death. It was not that she did not feel herself deserving of eternal punishment. On the contrary she used to say,—"what must that blood be worth that can purchase so bright an inheritance for a hell-deserving sinner like me!" Still the simplicity of her faith was such that she never seemed to dream of uncertainty about the future. She felt that the Spirit had sealed her with the adoption of a child, and as soon would she have doubted that Jesus had died, as that heaven was her home, and that a place was prepared for her there, to which death was but the entrance. She often asked to have the 14th chapter of John read to her, and delighted to apply its promises to herself. She dwelt with delight on that sweet expression *"sleeping in Jesus,"* and often repeated the hymn—

"Asleep in Jesus! blessed sleep—"
also that simple verse—

"Jesus can make a dying bed,
Feel soft as downy pillows are;
While on his breast I lean my head,
And breathe my life out sweetly there."

There were times when the recollection of the sins of her childhood cast a cloud over her spirit, but a brief one, quickly dispelled by a sight of the cross; and even this was not latterly permitted to trouble her. She told me one day how some particular sin, a lie, or act of disobedience long past, would appear before her in all its guilt, as "the abominable thing which God *hates*." "But," she added, repeating part of a hymn she constantly referred to—

"'There is a fountain filled with blood,'

and I must not forget that I was washed in it. I dare not think I have a sin too bad for that precious blood to wash away."

She told me, "In the beginning of my first illness I had days and nights of misery, with a conviction of unpardoned sin, and wearied to show my heart to my minister, and ask him what I should do to be saved. I had not courage for this, but I showed my black heart to the comforting Spirit, who led me straight to Jesus, and there loosed me from my burden. Ever since," she continued, "I have been led by the cords of love, in green pastures and beside still waters, and who shall separate me from the love of Christ?"

This text was oftener quoted by her than any other; she said her heart rested on it many a time even in her sleep, and she constantly awoke with it on her lips. Indeed the whole chapter in which it occurs (Rom. viii.) was a great favourite, and often read or heard by her.

One day when I came in, the traces of tears were on her face, and on my inquiring the cause of her sorrow, she said, "I've been sinful and ungrateful this morning, and that makes me sad. I was very weak for want of something, and wearied while mother was getting some tea ready. When she brought it, I took it, and forgot in my hurry to give thanks. I did it as soon as I minded, but was not it ungrateful? And God so good to me, and me so unworthy! It has been a sore grief to me, but I'm just bringing it to the same blood that has washed away my other sins." Next day she said, "I hope it has done me good, for I now feel lower than ever in myself, but sure there is forgiveness with God that he may be feared. While I'm in danger of forgetting on my quiet bed that I'm a sinful creature in the midst of sin and temptation, still this has shown me I must watch every moment, and come always back again to wash in the blood in which I washed before." Her tenderness of conscience was shown in many other instances, which it is impossible now to enumerate.

Emily was much in earnest about the souls of all around her, and used to pray and entreat Christian friends to pray, that she might so suffer and so die as to glorify God. She one day took the opportunity of our being alone to say, "I've a great favour to ask of you. When I am gone and need your visits no more, will you still sometimes come and speak of Jesus to those that are left?" On this occasion also, she referred particularly to her early days of wandering from God, and to the many times he knocked at her door, and she refused to hear. She said, "I was but a weakly lassie, and I never thought I was to be a long liver. Whenever I heard a discourse on death, I thought it was for me; and often when I went out or came in, and had to stand at the stairfoot to get breath, I trembled, thinking how soon my fluttering breath would stop altogether, and me not fit to meet the Judge." She added, "This thought often made me grave, while my companions in the workroom were all merry. I think now, it was the Holy Spirit stirring in me; but you see he had to knock louder yet, to bid me hear his voice, I was so hard to win." Many of the precious things she said have escaped my memory; but I shall never forget the expressive winding up of her little account of herself, when, nearly exhausted, she closed her eyes, fervently and distinctly, though very slowly uttering the words, "Now, my Beloved is mine, and I am his."

She sent an earnest message to the Bible class and another through Miss Withrow to her old class-fellows in the Sabbath-school. "Tell them," she said, "to seek Christ early, and not trust to a death-bed. Though he has given me twenty weeks, he may not give them one." She added, "Often have I grieved that I did not seek Christ sooner." She frequently sent for some of her young friends to her bed-side, and used her feeble strength in telling them what great things Christ had done for her soul, and what he would do for theirs, if they would taste his grace. She told me, "at first when anybody came in, I used to hold my tongue, I was so afraid to speak: but then I thought I might have short time to say a word for my Saviour, so I used to lift a prayer that God would take away my timidity, and teach me what to say. I think he has answered me, for often I've been helped to speak solemnly, though I was all shaking at the beginning."

One of her most intimate companions used often to go to inquire for her in the mornings, and then she would name over the hymns she wished her to read or to hear her repeat, asking also to hear the passage of Scripture on which they were founded, read to her, and dwell with delight on her favourite portions. She frequently spoke to her personally and solemnly. One day especially she addressed her thus, "Oh, my heart is like to break when I think of the many wasted Sabbath evenings we've spent together, and how we've quenched the Spirit by our idle words, when we came from school. If I were well again, I would spend the time better than gathering flowers about the meadows." These recollections agitated her much. She earnestly exhorted her companion, by the pain it gave her to look back upon her frequent quenching of the Spirit, now on her dying-bed, never again to yield to such temptations, and to come to Jesus while in health.

It is impossible to repeat many of her words, but they will be long remembered, not only by her young friends, but by all the neighbours who were in the habit of seeing her. Many of them spoke of her often with tears, some saying, "O for a deathbed like Emily's!" Others said, "Even when she could not speak, there was something about that child as good as a sermon."

None but those who previously knew Emily, and had marked her extreme timidity and reserve, can understand how doubly touching each word of simple faith and love which she uttered was to her friends. All old things had passed away with her, and truly even in the smallest things, all things seemed to have become new.

God took an instrument which for fourteen years had sounded only to the strains of earth, and transformed it to a heavenly harp, ere the silver cord was loosed; and when the blessed Spirit breathed over its strings, sweetly did they vibrate to the glory of the Redeemer, the melody becoming more full, more sweet, when the swellings of Jordan were deepest, and the everlasting hills were nearest. It was the Lord's doing, and wondrous in our eyes. Not for her praise, but for his glory, would we record it. To him be all the praise.

On the 17th of December, three weeks before the end of her course, she became much worse, and thought herself dying. She then begged to have those friends who were used to visit her made aware of her situation. Her message to Miss Withrow was, "Tell her I am going to sleep in Jesus now." Through her, she sent a message full of grateful affection to the absent teacher, who, she said, had not cast her bread upon the waters of her heart in vain. She said, "Give her my love, and ask her to pray that the good Shepherd may support me and help me to glorify him in the dark valley;" adding, "He will, I know he will."

I saw her twice that day. The first time, her cough and breathlessness almost prevented her from doing more than signifying to me that there was peace within and hope above, by pointing first to her heart and then upwards. In the evening, I found her still gasping for breath, but able to whisper, "Still happy in Jesus!" She seemed revived by the sight of a friend at an unusual hour, and she was able before I left to ask for the particular passages she wished me to read, and in broken sentences, to repeat most of the 23rd Psalm. She was interrupted by such a fit of coughing as I hardly expected her to survive. When restored to quiet, she observed the tears of those around her, and said with a smile, "This is all love. One-half hour in glory will more than make up for it all."

I regret now that I took no note but in memory, of any of her remarks, as however interesting and satisfactory the remembrance of our many conversations is to myself, but a vague idea of them can be conveyed to others. A few of these may however be instructive.

On Sabbath morning the 20th, she expressed disappointment at still being here. She said, "Yesterday I was rejoicing to think that while you would be today assembled, listening to our dear minister, or praising God in the sanctuary, I should be singing the song of Moses and the Lamb, or listening to my Saviour's voice. I'm wearying to see Jesus; but his will be done." Next day she said, "Still here,—with longing to depart and be with Christ." When I was leaving her, she beckoned me back, and drew my ear close to her pillow, as she often did when she had something to say, which her parched lips could hardly articulate. "Pray for me," she said, "and ask Mr. Bonar to do so too. Pray for *patience*, for I need it much." I supposed she meant patience under suffering; but when I asked her if she was inclined to murmur at her pain, she replied quickly, "Oh no, ma'am,—you do not understand me. I'm so weary to be home; I'm afraid my wearying is sinful, and patience to wait God's time is what I want." All that week her parting request was, "pray that I may have patience, and may glorify God in the dark valley," or something similar.

One day she told me that in the night, when she slept none, but had been dozing, she thought herself in heaven. "It was all full of light," she said, "and such music as I never heard; and what struck me most was the bands of little children that I saw. Heaven seemed full of them, all clothed in white robes; and I saw your little one there. I looked about for Jesus, and I saw a person sitting on a great white throne, so drowned in brightness that I could not tell what he was like. And just as I thought I had gotten to his feet, I opened my eyes, and, O ma'am, I doubt I murmured, when I saw no light but the dim light of the candle beside my bed!"

I reminded her how Jesus must have longed, when on earth, to return to his Father's bosom, and of the words, "O that I had the wings of a dove! then would I fly away and be at rest." "Aye," she said, "he hated sin and loved holiness as I can never do, and yet he said, 'not my will but thine be done.'" This passage seemed to comfort her greatly, and she told me afterwards that she now felt willing to wait God's time, and that "to live would be Christ to her, if she could but do a little for his glory."

She said, "Teach little Sarah a text of three words, which I hope she will love as I do, 'God is love;' and tell her I thought I saw her there." She told me she used often to meet that little one, but hung back shyly; while her companions who knew the attendant spoke to her. "But," she said, "I could not hear her sweet voice lisping about 'Gentle Jesus,' and 'Come unto me,' without tears. I used to think, 'O could I but be her keeper, and hear such sweet words every day, and be instructed by them that teach her, *it would be easy to be good!*' But ma'am, I did not know my own heart, and you see God has had another school to teach me in, and he has been my teacher."

One day, after a severe fit of coughing, her reply to an expression of sympathy was, "It's nothing to what Christ bore for me. He died upon the cross for me." At another time when asked if the pain was great, "Oh no; it's only breathlessness. It seems nothing at all when I think on Jesus' sufferings!" She used to say, "Oh, I am thirsty, but Jesus was thirsty." She took a deep interest in a young lady whom I mentioned to her as having in her the seeds of the same disease, which was rapidly destroying her young life, without possessing the same hope for the life to come. Again and again she inquired for her, "Does she know her complaint? Does she not think of the change of her soul? Is she not seeking Jesus yet?" She made her a subject of constant prayer.

On the last day of the year she expressed great fear of the sounds of revelry and profanity which she dreaded to hear from the streets that night. When I next saw her, she said, "I was grieved by what I heard; so different from the song, 'Worthy is the Lamb,' in which I had hoped to join the blessed above, ere new year's morning; but it just stirred me up to pray for the poor world lying in wickedness, and to give thanks that I am taken, while so many are left. I thought too how Jesus must have shrunk from sin, and how he would feel when he wept over Jerusalem." She said to those who brought their congratulations to her bedside, "Last new year's day I was running about with the other girls getting my cakes, but I would not exchange my dying bed for all their new year's mirth." She repeated one of her hymns, "I was a wandering sheep," saying it just described what she had been, and what grace had done for her.

Throughout the last week of her life, the blood of Christ seemed more dear to her than ever. She would say, "O it must be precious, if it can make such a heart as mine as white as snow." The two hymns oftenest on her lips were, "There is a fountain filled with blood," and "I lay my sins on Jesus." Two lines which occur in the latter hymn, were often whispered by her, as expressing her heart's desire, when she had not breath to say more,

"White in his blood most precious,
Till not a spot remains."

161

To a young friend who accompanied me to see her two or three days before her death, she spoke with affectionate solemnity, telling her how sweet it was to die in Jesus, and asking her, "Are you a fellow-traveler to the kingdom? Shall I see you there?" We were affected by her parting words that day, "Farewell till we meet in glory."

The next day her conversation was of a very interesting nature, though she seemed much weaker, and it was only audible close to her pillow. She spoke much of the home to which she was hastening, and of the blessed company which she was so soon to join. She said, "The thought of meeting Abraham, and Daniel, and the beloved John, has often given me songs in the night; but there's not a thought like this, 'forever with the Lord!'" She repeated some lines, which she said exactly expressed her feeling:

"Sweet Jesus! when I think of thee,
My heart for joy doth leap in me;
Thy blest remembrance yields delight,
But far more sweet will be thy sight."

In reply to some remark on her having been continued here so much longer than she had anticipated, she said, "Oh, how I wearied for my home, when I saw it so near me. It was a sore struggle to make up my mind to stop away from my Saviour any longer, but *now* I am quite willing to bide till he sends for me; *now* I can say, 'Even so, Father.'" When asked, if she could see any purpose for which God had prolonged her life, she said, "Aye, that is made plain to me. Even if for nothing else it has been a blessed time to my own soul. It has been a *teaching* time. Each day that has been added to my life has added to my knowledge of my God. Each day he has been enlarging my heart, and revealing more of his own goodness and love to me. I bless him that I can say, 'I know him better than I did three weeks ago.'" Was not this a delightful testimony for one so young! I felt she had indeed been ripening fast for glory under his wise dealings with her, and I went away saying, "I thank thee, O Father, Lord of heaven and earth, because thou hast hidden these things from the wise and prudent, and revealed them unto babes."

Next day, I saw dear Emily for the last time, and a change in her countenance, and an unusual dullness in her eyes, together with occasional incoherence, all told that the last enemy was very near. She was able to speak little, but that little was very sweet. "Still happy in Jesus" was even now her feeble greeting. She felt pained to be less able to fix her mind than formerly, but she said, "I think the Spirit was helping my infirmities when Mr. Bonar was praying with me. I hardly lost a word of that prayer, and O, it was sweet! I've been praying for him whenever I could since; he has much on his hands and much on his mind, but he will be strengthened, and he will have a rich reward."

She said something, in an unconnected way, about flowers. I said, "If the snow were not so deep, Emily, you should not wish for flowers in vain, could any be found." "It's not that, ma'am,—

> 'There everlasting spring abides;
> And never withering flowers.'

I'll soon see the Rose of Sharon and the Lily of the Valley, for there's no snow yonder."

These words were accompanied by the last gleam that I saw in her dying eyes. The cough continued very bad during the night, till within a few minutes of her release. About half-past four she said she could not see, and asked if the candle was out. Her last breath was spent in repeating a great part of the hymn; "I lay my sins on Jesus," but weakness prevented her finishing it. It was said, "You will soon be with Jesus now, Emily." "I know that," she said quietly, closing her eyes, as if for sleep, and without a sigh, this young disciple "fell asleep in Jesus."

My dear young readers, when you lay down this little book, I hope you will not be satisfied with merely wishing you were like Emily. What will that avail you, if it does not lead you to your Saviour's feet, to seek for his name's sake, pardon and holiness as well as heaven?

Do you envy Emily's calm endurance of suffering? Do you envy her happy deathbed? Do you envy the joy unspeakable and full of glory to which she often looked forward, and which is now eternally her own? Then hasten to acquaint yourselves with Emily's God. Do not linger because you are young; so was she. Do not linger because you think you are more disobedient, more deceitful, more full of sin than she; not so. If she were here she would tell you that such was she. "But she is washed, but she is sanctified, but she is justified in the name of the Lord Jesus, and by the Spirit of our God."

I LAY MY SINS ON JESUS

I lay my sins on Jesus,
The spotless Lamb of God;
He bears them all, and frees us
From the accursed load.
I bring my guilt to Jesus,
To wash my crimson stains
White in His blood most precious,
Till not a spot remains.

I lay my wants on Jesus,
All fullness dwells in Him;
He heals all my diseases,
He doth my soul redeem
I lay my griefs on Jesus,
My burdens and my cares;
He from them all releases,
He all my sorrows shares.

I rest my soul on Jesus,
This weary soul of mine;
His right hand me embraces,
I on his breast recline.
I love the name of Jesus,
Immanuel, Christ, the Lord;
Like fragrance on the breezes,
His name abroad is poured.

I long to be like Jesus—
Meek, loving, lowly, mild;
I long to be like Jesus,
The Father's holy child.
I long to be with Jesus,
Amid the heavenly throng,
To sing, with saints, His praises,
To learn the angels' song.

THE END